JUSTICE
in Jackson

D1565297

by
Phil Hardwick

QUAIL RIDGE PRESS
Brandon, Mississippi

Other books in Phil Hardwick's Mississippi Mysteries Series:

Found in Flora
Captured in Canton
Newcomer in New Albany
Vengeance in Vicksburg
Collision in Columbia
Conspiracy in Corinth

To be included on the Mississippi Mysteries mailing list,
please send your name and complete mailing address to:

QUAIL RIDGE PRESS
P. O. Box 123 • Brandon, MS 39043
1-800-343-1583

DEDICATION

This book is dedicated to
those men and women of law enforcement
who put on a uniform every workday.

Preface / Acknowledgments

The author thanks those who provided editorial assistance and advice: Bob, Carol, Chip, Dennis, and Michele. A special thanks to Murray Wilson, who is the real owner of Jack Boulder's Camaro.

SUNDAY

Chapter 1

The best and worst thing I ever did in my life was kill Harvey Waverly.

It was the worst thing because I took another person's life. Nobody has the right to kill someone else, unless it's to save another life. On the other hand, it was the best thing I ever did, because it took me out of a job I was beginning to despise, made me a lot of money, and has allowed me to live the kind of life I want to live, not what someone else or circumstance dictates. It also brought justice to a situation where too often injustice prevails.

I guess all this takes some explaining, so here goes.

My name is Jack Boulder. Actually, it's Andrew Jackson Boulder. A couple of years ago I was a detective lieutenant in Homicide on the St. Louis, Missouri Police Department. I worked in the streets of one of the toughest areas of the Gateway City. I thought I could make a difference where it counted. Much of the time, I did just that.

One day, my partner Andy Smith didn't show up for work. We called his house and got no answer, so the Chief of Detectives asked me to go check on him. When I parked the unmarked police cruiser in his driveway, I knew something was wrong. I have this sixth sense that tells me when things are not as they should be. I went to the front door of his modest two-story house and knocked. Getting no answer, I went to the storage room and retrieved the extra key from behind the deep freezer. I let myself into the house and found Andy, his wife, Debbie, and their 6-year old little girl, Mandy, each dead from a bullet wound. Andy and his wife were just lying there in bed. Mandy was sprawled out on the floor of the hall, still wearing her pajamas. She probably heard the shots that killed her mommy and daddy, and came to investigate. None of them ever had a chance.

Two weeks later, a tip to the crime hotline led to an arrest. The perpetrator was a four-time convicted ex-con of human scum named Harvey Waverly. He confessed to breaking into the house and killing them with a 9mm pistol he had stolen from a local pawn shop. He said he was glad to have wasted a cop, and would do it again. I couldn't take that.

On the day of Waverly's arraignment I waited for him in the hallway that connected the jail to the court-house. When he came by, he looked me straight in the eye and uttered in a raspy, animal-like voice, "What are you going to do about it, pig?" I put six bullets into the chest of Harvey Waverly. He would never kill anyone again.

I was immediately arrested and charged with murder by a district attorney who was running for state attorney general. After a three-day trial, the jury announced that it was hopelessly deadlocked and the judge declared a mistrial. The publicity involved with the case was very positive toward me, and I became a symbol of the need for some people to take the law into their own hands. National newspapers interviewed me and I was a guest on two national morning news shows.

During the trial, I sat at the table and thought about Harvey Waverly and what would have happened to him if I hadn't shot him. He would serve four or five years and be back out on the street to do it all over. I thought about what I would have done if that had happened. I counted the ways I would make Harvey Waverly's remaining life miserable. On the second day of the trial, I started writing those ways down on paper. Things like putting sugar in his gas tank, ordering items delivered to his home, nails under his tires, annoying telephone calls, police calls to his house, phony credit report information, and a hundred other ways to bug the you-know-what out of him. On the third day, a newspaper reporter asked me what I was writing. I showed him, and he loved it. He took it to a publisher, and by the end of the trial, it was announced that *Jack Boulder's 121 Ways To Get Even* would be published to help defray my legal expenses. I signed a contract with the publisher giving me a royalty on each book sold. I got about one dollar per book. In the first month 12,000 copies were sold in the St. Louis area. The second month it went national, and sold well for over a year. I reported $244,000 in taxable income to Uncle Sam that year.

In short, the D.A. did not re-indict, and then lost the election, probably because of public opinion against indicting me in the first place. Although I became a celebrity in St. Louis, I decided it was not the right place for me. I took early retirement from the police department and moved back to my boyhood home of Jackson, Mississippi. I paid cash for a new three-bedroom condo at Capitol Place, in the heart of downtown. I have this thing about not wanting to be indebted to anyone for anything.

Capitol Place is a twenty-unit complex located across the street from Smith Park. It had been built two years ago by a developer who believed there was a market for quality downtown housing. There were many who said such a project was folly. The developer had the last laugh when every single unit sold out before construction was completed. The place has a strong New Orleans French Quarter flavor, complete with bricked courtyard and a flowing fountain in the middle. I'm the second owner of my unit, a prime, two-story model that overlooks the park. On the first level is a living room, dining room, kitchen, half-bath and a large bedroom that serves as my office. The windows on the street side are small, for security purposes, but the French doors on the second level open onto a large balcony over Congress Street. There is another set of doors and balcony that open onto the interior courtyard.

The Mississippi Governor's Mansion is less than fifty yards across the way, and the State Capitol is one hundred yards to the north. Just last week, while having coffee one morning in the sidewalk café down the block, I heard a couple from South America remark that they had visited the capitol buildings of every state in the U.S. and found Mississippi's capitol building to be the most beautiful. I could not disagree. It is a masterpiece. Jacksonians need only to visit a few other state capitols to really appreciate what they have.

I'm divorced with no kids, so I don't have a lot of expenses. My income is derived from three sources. First, there is the retirement check from the police department. Second, the book royalties allow me to put a little money in the bank, but I know that income won't

last forever. Third, I hung out my shingle as a private detective. Business was slow, at first, because I was still getting reacquainted with my old hometown. But now, with each new case comes a client who is a potential referral for more new business. I also renewed acquaintances with a high school girlfriend—but more about that later. My office contains state-of-the-art computer equipment. I admit to spending entirely too much time on the Internet, but it is a terrific research tool. If people only knew what could be discovered about them on the Internet, they would be amazed and probably frightened. I have a home page on the "net" for people who want to find out a little more about my services.

So, that's who I am, where I am, and what I do. If I had known what was going to happen during the coming week in my life, I don't know if I would have returned to Jackson, Mississippi.

Chapter 2

It was a typical June evening in the hot and humid South, the air hanging heavy, hazy, and damp over downtown Jackson. I made myself a gin and tonic, opened the French doors and stepped outside to my balcony perched above the sidewalk of Congress Street below. I sat in an iron patio chair and gazed up and past Smith Park, past the spire of St. Peter's Cathedral, to the top floor of the Deposit Guaranty Plaza Building. The golden ceiling lights of the University Club chandeliers twinkled above the twenty-one floors of dark plate glass below it. It was about 10:00 p.m. Sunday evening. Tomorrow the offices behind those black windows would come alive with bankers, lawyers, and business people making their loans, suing each other, and making deals. I was glad I wasn't a part of that rat race. My office was in my home, in bedroom number three.

Ten city blocks past the University Club is west central Jackson, an area that has seen better days. Drug dealers rule the streets there now. The decent people who remain are virtually prisoners in their own homes. Those who report suspicious activity to the police receive a quick visit from representatives of a local gang who deliver the threat in businesslike fashion—"Call the police again, and your house will burn down." Burned-out houses in the neighborhood merely add to the validity of the threat. It takes only one visit.

I took another sip of my gin and tonic and thought that at this very minute, there were probably a dozen street deals going on. Some would lead to heated arguments, and a few would lead to homicide. In west central Jackson, killing another person who "disses" you is justifiable homicide. I'm glad I don't have to respond to the sorting-out of who shot whom and why anymore. I've seen enough bloody, dying teenagers in my career as a police officer to realize that I can't solve society's inner city problems. I decided that I didn't even want to watch the ten o'clock news tonight. It was always the same: scene one—a body loaded into an ambulance, cut to a reporter standing in front of yellow police "do not cross" tape; scene two—reports of a scandal in government; scene three—residents cleaning up a neighborhood to make it a better place to live. This was the late evening news format not only in Jackson, Mississippi, but just about every top 100 TV market in the United States.

Unknown to me, at that very moment, a street deal was about to take place at the corner of Central and Prentiss Streets. Derrick James and Rodney Johnson, two local thugs with arrest records longer than the Pearl River, jumped off the porch of the vacant house on which they had been sitting and ran up to the driver's window of a silver van that had pulled up to the curb. Derrick made a motion with his right hand for the driver to roll down his window. As he did so, the window was powered down by the white man inside the vehicle. It was not unusual to see white people on this corner in the middle of an African-American neighborhood. "Whitey" came here all the time to buy his drugs. Derrick and Rodney were only too happy to supply what was needed. After all, it put good money in their pockets and helped finance the activities of their small, but growing, gang.

"What you got?" said the driver.

Derrick quickly replied that he had whatever the man wanted—crack, coke or ludes. Rodney kept his eyes on the streets in case trouble or another customer should come by.

The sliding side door of the van opened and a deep male voice from inside said, "Come here and let's see." Derrick stuck his head inside the door and felt strong, gloved hands go around his right arm and yank him inside. Rodney turned around as Derrick's shoes disappeared into the darkness of the van.

"Hey man, what's going on?"

Even though his street sense told him something was wrong, Rodney also stuck his head inside the van and was swallowed up inside. The van drove away at normal speed, leaving the corner deserted. Within eight minutes, drug dealers Derrick and Rodney had been replaced by two more entrepreneurs of the drug world.

I drained the last of my drink, said good night to downtown, and went to bed.

MONDAY

Chapter 3

I woke up early Monday morning, did a few stretching exercises and headed out for my usual morning run
up State Street to Millsaps College and back. When I
returned, I did thirty minutes of weights in the Capitol
Place exercise room. This daily ritual allowed me to
maintain my weight of one hundred eighty-eight
pounds, exactly what I tipped the scales at on the day I
graduated from the police academy twenty-one years
ago. After shaving and getting dressed, I headed out to
my only appointment of the day. Last Friday afternoon,
I had received a telephone call from Alvin Porter, owner
of Porter Direct Goods, a catalogue merchandiser with
corporate offices in the IOF Building in downtown
Jackson. Porter made it clear to me that his call had
nothing to do with his company, but instead had something to do with the Jackson Business Association.

At 8:45 a.m., I walked out from my condo onto the
interior courtyard, locking the door behind me. The
humidity instantly enveloped me—another usual summer day in the South. It didn't bother me, however,
because I was wearing my now normal work uniform of
khaki slacks, polo shirt, and walking loafers. It still
amazes me that people dress in coats and ties in a cli-
mate like this. They could learn something from the

Hawaiians, who know how to dress business casual.

I exited the courtyard on the Smith Park side and turned left on Congress Street. As I did so, I looked over my shoulder at the State Capitol Building and said a mental good morning to Gertrude, the gold eagle that sits atop the building. Gertrude faces to the south, that fact supposedly having something to do with the Civil War. Gertrude is the name I gave her, but she may be a Heathcliff. In any event she watches over downtown Jackson—and me.

Two blocks of walking the sidewalk alongside brick-paved Congress Street took me to the IOF Building, formerly known as Capitol Towers. In days past it was the site of the City Auditorium, home of everything from formal evening dances to "rasslin" matches. Today's more contemporary civic auditorium is located one block over, on Pascagoula Street. It is now Thalia Mara Hall, named in honor of the famous ballet teacher from New York who helped to bring the International Ballet Competition's USA site to Jackson, Mississippi. The event is held every four years for several weeks during the summer, and transforms Jackson into an international city. Speaking of international events, abiding on the same block is the Mississippi Arts Center, where international exhibits such as the Palaces of St. Petersburg and Splendors of Versailles are held.

I took the IOF building elevator to the fifteenth floor offices of my prospective client. After a short wait in a carpeted reception room decked out in Currier & Ives prints, I was ushered in to see the boss by a secretary who dressed like she was still living in the 1950s.

"Have a seat, Mr. Boulder," beckoned Alvin Porter, president of the Jackson Business Association. He looked about five foot eleven, late fifties, hair with hues of blonde, gold and brown. Actually, his hair looked like hay straw. He had a good tan. I'm not sure if I would describe him as portly or pudgy—he was filled out, but not really fat. He looked like someone who lived the good life and was outside a lot, but not active. A gold wedding band on his left ring finger was so tight, I doubted that he could get it off if he needed to. The room had dark paneling on three sides, and a full glass wall on the other. The view was to the east, and all you could see were the backs of other downtown buildings. On one wall was a collection of plaques from business organizations, on another was a grouping of framed, enlarged photographs of a large pleasure boat, and behind his desk was a print of a deer jumping a fence in a snow-covered meadow. Somehow it did not all go together very well. He sat behind his executive desk, a piping hot cup of coffee in front of him. He did not offer me a cup.

"I'll get right to the point, Mr. Boulder," he said. "We have a crisis in our community, and many people think that the police are responsible. Some even say that one of our mayoral candidates is involved."

"What are you referring to?" I asked.

"For the past three weeks, a series of disappearances has been occurring. The victims, if they can be called that, are some of Jackson's biggest criminals—mostly drug dealers. It's as if overnight they just left town. Things like that don't just happen," he said.

"And who's complaining about that?"

"Some upset mamas, for starters. Today they are going to publicly demand that the FBI be called in to investigate. Standing beside those grieving mothers will be none other than the illustrious Timothy Tyler. It will be a golden opportunity for a liberal like him to advance his candidacy on the backs of poor folks. No doubt he'll talk about the rights of the children who have been kidnapped, and how, once again, the police department is letting down the community. It's going to make the police look very bad. As a matter of fact, some people actually think the police are doing the kidnapping."

"Why would the police want to do that?"

"So the crime problem will go down. Or go away. The public is fed up with crime."

"Every large city in the country has a crime problem," I pointed out.

"True," he replied, pointing a finger at me. "But this is Jackson. Many people who grew up here remember when Jackson was considered one of the safest cities in the world. They remember not locking their doors at night. Now they are afraid that they are losing the

Jackson they once knew. Hell, man, haven't you seen the billboards lately? There are pawn shops galore, developers telling you to get out of town and security companies reminding you of a national crime ranking. That's not the Jackson many people grew up in."

"I see."

He went on to tell me that the position of his association—at least in the immediate future—is to support the police and let them do their work. He said that the JBA had just raised a quarter of a million dollars to buy new state-of-the-art crime-fighting equipment for the police department. It was time that businesses started supporting the police, instead of threatening to move out of town. It would not look very good if the police were involved in some scandalous activity at this time. He also explained that the JBA was not the Chamber of Commerce. His group was a collection of business people who were concerned with political and governmental affairs. He would only allow that there were "hundreds" of members. He smiled coyly, and said that I would be surprised at how many Jacksonians "get their kicks from pol-i-tics."

I looked him straight in the eye, raised my eyebrows, and asked him if HE thought the police were doing the kidnapping. He lowered his eyes, picked up his cup of coffee and took a sip. In my experience, that kind of action indicates that he was either about to lie, or didn't believe what he was about to say.

"God help us if they are," he said setting the cup back down. "But the business community has got to find out. That's where you come in. We need an outside, third party to look into this, and reassure everyone that neither the police department nor any of its members, is involved. You come highly recommended."

"With all due respect, Mr. Porter, you're asking me to prove a negative. I recall my high school science teacher telling me that was impossible."

He could not disagree with the logic. Nevertheless, I understood his problem. I quoted a fee that left plenty of room for contingencies, and told him that I might need help in setting up some interviews.

"I'll take care of that, for sure," he said. "Now, if you'll excuse me, I have a meeting in the conference room."

Chapter 4

As I rode the elevator back down to the ground floor, I considered the implications of this case. If there was a group of police officers kidnapping criminals, then this town had the potential to come apart. Vigilante justice cannot be tolerated in a free society. Ha! Listen to me—that's exactly what I represent to some people. Perhaps I should go back up and tell Mr. Porter to find someone else.

As the elevator door opened, I decided to walk across the way and venture inside City Hall. I had never been inside the building, and knew nothing of its history. Lately, it was famous for the boisterous City Council meetings that went on there. As I walked inside the foyer, I saw that there were approximately twenty people in the hallway. There was a flurry of activity. As I entered the hallway and peered through the windowed doors to the Council Chamber, it was obvious that the regular 10:00 a.m. City Council meeting was about to begin. I really did not want any part of this show, so I wandered around inspecting the public portion of the building. I picked up a brochure about City Hall and learned a few things.

Jackson, like many state capitals, began as a government city. When Mississippi was admitted to statehood in 1817, the center of commerce in the state was Natchez, on the Mississippi River. The first capital was

actually in that vicinity, in a little town called Washington. One of the first things the state Legislature did was to appoint a committee of three to recommend a permanent site for the location of the seat of state government. Jackson had three things going for it: it was near the Natchez Trace, the Nashville to Natchez overland trail route; it was near the geographic center of the state; and it was on the Pearl River at the site of an active trading post, known as LeFleur's Bluff. The hero of the day was Major General Andrew Jackson, so the city, just like me, was named after him.

It was indeed appropriate that the city was named for the man who would become the seventh President of the United States, and simultaneously, the best-loved and most-hated president the young country had ever known. "Old Hickory" was the first poor boy to become President. He also founded a modern political party (the Democrats). The little guys—frontier people, farmers, small businessmen, and workers—loved him.

Unlike some of the thirty-six cities in the United States named Jackson, the City of Jackson, Mississippi had a real connection with the man. Major Thomas Hinds, one of the aforementioned committee of three, had led a battalion of Mississippi Territory soldiers alongside General Jackson in battle against the Indians in 1813, and the British, in the Battle of New Orleans. The general visited his Mississippi namesake on more than one occasion. He made a stop while campaigning for President, and again in January of 1840, when he was a feeble retired President on a trip to celebrate the twenty-fifth anniversary of the Battle of New Orleans. No doubt he made other stops, because he visited Natchez frequently. Indeed, he was married there.

The City Hall building was completed in 1847 for a total construction cost of $7,505.58, no doubt kept low by the use of skilled slave craftsmen. The second floor was the meeting place for the Oddfellows and the Freemasons, both of which helped with the cost of construction. I glanced up the stairway to the second floor landing and saw bronze plaques on the walls commemorating those organizations. It is said that the reason City Hall escaped the torch during the Civil War was because General Sherman of the Union Army was a Mason. Perhaps it was because of its use as a hospital.

The building was spared, in any event, which is more than can be said for the rest of the city. It was burned on three occasions during the conflict, hence its nickname of "Chimneyville."

I walked back outside and strolled around Josh Halbert Gardens, a beautiful half-block of trimmed shrubbery, magnolia trees, colorful flowers, and brick walkways. I paused and read a marker.

Josh Halbert Gardens is a tribute to one man's unusual service to his city over a period of more than half a century. Long time City Engineer, director of public works, park designer and contributor to Jackson's beauty. This park lives for the enjoyment of the people of Jackson, their friends and our guests. In the midst of a busy city it provides a small place of beauty for each of us to pause a moment and reflect on man's ingenuity, possible by the grace of God.

I took a seat on a metal bench beside a larger-than-life statue of General Jackson. He stands in military uniform in the center of the garden at the head of a flowing stream of water.

I gazed across Pascagoula Street to the Hinds County Courthouse building and its statues of Moses the Lawgiver and Solomon the Wise Judge standing stately on opposite sides of the roof. Hundreds of Jacksonians pass by every day, never realizing that Moses is looking down on them. It's funny how people, myself included, never see things right before their eyes. I glanced back up at Moses, and wondered silently if there was justice in Jackson.

As if in response to that thought, my gaze turned diagonally toward the headquarters of the Jackson Police Department. On top of its roof were several radio antennae. Its four-story, concrete functionality stood in contrast to the grace and beauty of City Hall. Might as well begin this case at the source of concern.

I walked over to the police department headquarters building, and up to the top floor office of Deputy Chief of Police, Tom Dallas. Tom and I graduated from high school one year apart, he ahead of me. After serving a hitch in the Army, including a combat-decorated tour of Vietnam, he returned to Jackson and joined the police department. Once he obtained his degree in criminal justice, he rose quickly up the ladder and became deputy chief three years ago. He was, as they say, a good man. Although it would not be fully correct to say that we were close personal friends, we were good acquaintances.

His secretary showed me into his office without checking with him. He got up from his neatly arranged desk and reached out his big paw of a hand. He stood six-foot-three and weighed every bit of two hundred twenty-five pounds. His hair was thinning on top, and his temples were turning gray. He wore the white shirt of a high-ranking officer; there were three gold stars on his collar. I noticed a copy of my book on his credenza, in the middle of a collection of police administration and criminal law texts.

"Sit down, Jack. Alvin Porter called me and informed me that the business association has hired you to prove that the police aren't involved." He leaned forward, and placed his elbows on the desktop. "We appreciate what JBA does for the department, and I want you to know that you've got anything you need from us."

"Thanks, Tom. I really appreciate it. Can you give me a quick briefing?"

He removed a file jacket from the left hand side of the desk and laid it in front of him. It was about an inch thick, and contained lots of looseleaf papers, many of which were attached to each other with paper clips. He referred to the file as he explained that three weeks ago, the department received a report of a missing person. There was no evidence of kidnapping, but the person who made the report—the victim's sister—was convinced that her seventeen-year-old brother had been kidnapped and murdered. The sister was nineteen years old and had a factory job. She freely admitted what the police already knew—that her brother, Luther Weaver, was a drug dealer and gang member. Even so, she said, he called her every day, and she hadn't heard from him. The police had opened a case and put out the word that they were looking for Luther. Dallas said he expected to find an unidentified body that would later be determined to be Luther.

A week later, a funny thing happened. Officers on the street begin noticing that the regular drug dealers weren't on their customary corners. Dallas said that they also noticed something else—crime was going down at a time of year when it usually went up. More missing person reports had come in. Every victim had an extensive criminal record and had served time. The department now had a total of seven such reports. It was as if Jackson's most notorious criminals were disappearing from the face of the earth.

Dallas went on to say that he believed there may be as many as fifteen street dealers who had vanished—or whatever. Yes, he conceded that it was possible that a few rogue cops were playing vigilante, but he had no proof, or even a reasonable suspicion to go on. He reiterated that anything I needed was mine, because the thing needed to be handled fast. It was about to become a political issue, what with the mayor's race going on. I thanked him and told him that I would be in touch.

Chapter 5

I left the police department through a side door that opened onto Congress Street, took a left, and walked past the *Clarion-Ledger,* Jackson's daily newspaper. At Pearl Street I took another left, and continued a block and a half to the rear entrance of the Edison Walthall Hotel. I walked up a ramp through the parking garage, and entered a lobby lush with wood paneling.

As I walked through the automatic sliding glass doors, I was transformed from urban streets into the world of fine hotels, where the brass is polished regularly and the mahogany receives a loving touch. Off the hallway, a small library invited me to stop, select a good book off the shelf, and have a seat in one of the plush sofas. I resisted, but made a mental note to spend some time there one day in the near future. I strolled on, past the small gift shop on my left and the barber shop on my right. The coolness of the conditioned air reinvigorated me, as did my anticipation of meeting Laura Webster, attorney-at-law, for lunch. Laura and I had "gone steady" for a whole six months during our senior year of high school. That may not seem like a very long time to a middle-aged adult, but when one is in high school, six months is a very long time. Now, twenty-something years later, we had been reacquainted. She is a full partner in one of the law firms located in Deposit Guaranty Plaza. Over the years, both of us have had amazingly similar lives in two respects—short marriages and total commitment to our work.

Up ahead, I spied Laura standing at the entrance to the restaurant. She was engaged in conversation with the restaurant manager and had two fingers raised, indicating the number in her party. She was wearing a dark blue suit, accessorized with a red and white scarf. That meant she had probably been in a conference with a judge and another lawyer today. I had learned how to read her dress code, and she readily admitted that I had deciphered it accurately. There were three corporate versions of Laura. One was the trial lawyer who wore gray suits and white blouses, her hair in a bun. Another was the law researcher, who wore pant suits and her hair down. Then there was this one, the one who had meetings and conferences and dressed accordingly. She was quite a lady and I felt lucky to be her boyfriend. I suppose that word would describe our relationship.

When I was about fifteen feet away, she turned and saw me. A smile that would bring happiness to the heart of a depressed funeral home director crossed her face. After greeting each other with a hug, we were seated at a cloth-draped table for two, by a window that looked out onto Capitol Street.

"And how's your day going?" I asked.

"I can answer that after I get a ruling on the motion I filed this morning for a dismissal." She smiled, and took a sip of lemon water as I told the waitperson we would both have the buffet. "And what's your day doing for you?"

After making our way through a sumptuous buffet line, I told her about my meeting with Alvin Porter of the JBA and Deputy Chief Dallas of the Jackson Police Department.

"You know that you are being used, don't you?"

"How's that?" I replied.

"When the finger of blame is pointed at the police department, all it has to do is point to you," she said.

"My client is not the police department. It is the Jackson Business Association. Nobody will even know that I'm working on this."

"Jack, the sun won't rise over the Pearl River again without your name being mentioned in the media," she said profoundly as she took her first bite of the pecan pie on the table in front of her.

"Are you saying that I made a mistake?"

"Not at all," she said. "It's just not going to be as clean as you think. After all, there is a mayor's race going on."

I confess to turning a deaf ear to politics. I saw my share of political shenanigans in St. Louis, so I did not even try to keep up with the local politics in Jackson.

"I know there is a race. Tell me about the candidates."

"There are two. Timothy Tyler versus Walter B. Fox," she said, in the manner of a court clerk announcing the next case. "White liberal versus black conservative. It is a tight race that is too close to call. With the election coming up next Tuesday, anything can happen. Each of the candidates needs a break in order to swing it his way. I have a feeling that what you are going to be working on may be the break that one of them is going to get."

We talked on, and before we knew it, forty-five minutes had passed. I invited her to stop by my condo after work so that we could continue our discussion of the mayor's race. I wondered if I had made the right decision in taking on this case. I bid her good-bye, and took care of the bill. The attractive lady behind the register not only asked if everything was alright with our lunch, but she also sounded as if she really meant it. There really is something genuine about people in the South.

Chapter 6

Laura arrived at my condo at 5:45 p.m. I turned on the television and switched to a local station. The national network news anchor was still on the screen. I went to the wet bar and made Laura a scotch and water, which is my winter drink, and myself a gin and tonic, which is my summer drink. The national news signed off, and a promo for the local news came on the screen.

As Laura and I waited for the local newscast, a crowd of twenty people had gathered and lined up on the steps on the west side of City Hall, as if ready for a group photograph. In front of them was a wooden podium adorned with microphones from three local television stations and other news media. Television station vans stood parked in the driveway, with their antennae reaching skyward. Two television stations were preparing to "go live" at 6:01 p.m.

Susan Sanderson, local government reporter for WAPT-TV, stared intently at the small television monitor that lay on the ground six feet in front of her, waiting for the cue from the television station. Her cameraman spoke, "Ready to go live in three, two, one." He pointed his right index finger at her.

"We are live at City Hall in downtown Jackson where Timothy Tyler, one of two candidates for mayor of Jackson, is expected to appear momentarily to make a statement that we understand will have something to do with the police department." There was a commotion behind her, as the crowd parted and Tyler descended the steps and took his position behind the podium. He was wearing a blue denim shirt. "I see that Mr. Tyler has appeared. Let's see what he has to say."

The camera zoomed in for a head and shoulders shot. Tyler surveyed the reporters, pausing to look each one in the eye, and said, "I want you to take a good look at the five women on my right."

He gestured with his right arm fully extended. As a he did so, he knocked down one of the microphones in front of him. It fell to the asphalt, like a snake that had been shot. A young reporter scrambled down to his knees, retrieved the device, and replaced it in its holder on the podium. Tyler acted as if it had never happened.

"These women have sons who have been reported missing to the Jackson Police Department within the past two weeks. All of the victims are young men whom the Jackson Police Department could care less about. Young men who are gone. Young men who have yet to reach the prime of life. Where have they gone? But more importantly, does anybody care?"

There was a sob and a sniff from the runny nose of one of the women in the group. She was immediately comforted by the other women, who patted her on the back and told her that it was all right. Tyler continued his speech.

"Maybe you care. Maybe you don't. I'll tell you who does care and who does not care. The people up here on these steps care. The man behind this microphone cares." He raised his voice louder. "And I think the people of Jackson care. But it is obvious that our law enforcement community does not care. The Jackson Police Department does not care. They took a report—many reports—and just filed them away. Can you imagine that? Took a report and filed it. If five teenagers from the rich, northeast Jackson subdivision of Eastover had been reported missing in the past fourteen days, what do you think would be happening?" He let the words sink in. "I can tell you. The National Guard would have been called out, and search parties would have been organized."

"Now we must ask ourselves: Why is this happening? Why would the police department allow something like this to go on? There can only be one of two reasons—either they want it to happen, or else they are involved with it.

"Today, I am calling on the United States Justice Department to investigate the Jackson Police Department and expose its role in the disappearance of these young men."

He paused, looked up and waited for questions. His sudden ending caught some reporters unprepared.

"What evidence do you have that the Jackson Police Department is involved?" asked a newspaper reporter.

"The same evidence that is used in court—circumstantial evidence. Examine the circumstances, and it will be concluded that somehow the JPD is letting these families down."

"Are you suggesting a cover-up?" asked a WJTV reporter.

"Call it what you like. I am suggesting that the police department is not doing its job. Ask Chief Dallas to respond, and see what he says. The actions of his department are indefensible. As usual, I might add."

The head and shoulders of the anchor person in the television studio appeared on the screen. He looked serious and said, "And that's the report, live from City Hall. I'm sure we will have more on what may be a breaking story."

I picked up the remote control, aimed it at the television, pressed the power button and watched the color picture dissolve into dark, gray glass. Laura was right. This was going to get ugly. I needed all the information

I could get about the candidates, if for no other reason than my own self-protection.

Turning to Laura I said, "So, tell me what there is to know about Timothy Tyler and Walter B. Fox."

For the next forty minutes, she did so. Both men were born in Jackson. Both were running for mayor. That is where the similarities ended.

Timothy Tyler was a political consultant and all-around activist. Over the years, he had worked for just about every left wing cause that came along. From removing Christmastime crosses on government property to prohibiting prayer in public schools, he had been there. He was known as confrontational, but a seeker of legal means to redress grievances. He was grudgingly respected by those in government, because he was constitutionally correct most of the time.

Tyler and his older sister had been raised by their mother, who worked two jobs to make ends meet. Their father had deserted the family when Tyler was in the first grade. After graduating from the Jackson Public Schools, he got an associate degree from Hinds Community College. From there it was a stint in the Peace Corps. Upon his return to Jackson, he worked in every political campaign that came along, always for the most liberal candidate. He was married for five years, but it ended in divorce. There were no children. He was fond of saying, "It is never too late to make right the wrongs of the past."

Walter Bernard Fox, on the other hand, was a black attorney who was associated with Farmer, Wayson and Morris, one of the state's largest law firms. He was a full partner and head of the tax division. Educated in the public schools, he went on to the University of Virginia, where he played linebacker on the varsity football team and graduated in the top five percent of his class. Upon graduation, he was sought after by some of the country's most prestigious law firms. His father was a college professor, and his mother a housewife. He was married, had two children and lived in fashionable Eastover in northeast Jackson. He drove a new BMW and his two children attended an exclusive college preparatory school. He served on numerous boards, including the Jackson Business Association, and was active in community affairs, especially those that raised money for prevention of some disease. Tall and trim, he wore expensive suits and turned heads every time he walked into a room. His favorite political slogan was, "The only color is green."

"Would you now care to hear the latest poll results?" asked Laura.

"I'm all ears."

"Tyler has forty-eight percent of the white vote, and forty-eight percent of the black vote, with the rest undecided."

"What about Fox?" I inquired.

"Exact same percentages. Just the other side of the

political coin," she said.

The telephone rang. Unfortunately, I answered with my name. It was Dennis Davis, Channel 3 News.

Chapter 7

"Mr. Boulder," began the man who was known as Jackson's top investigative news reporter, "we're working on a story for the ten o'clock news about Timothy Tyler's allegations that the police department might be involved in the disappearance of several Jackson teenagers . . ."

"What does that have to do with me?" I interrupted.

"We understand that you have been hired by the police department to prove that wrong," he said.

I knew from the question that this was no average reporter. If I denied it, he would ask who hired me. If I said "yes" to his question, he immediately had a story. I needed to buy some time.

"How do I know who you are?"

"Call the WLBT news line listed in the telephone book, and see who answers," he said.

I looked at Laura, who was now leaning forward in her chair. She had deduced that this was a call from the media. I needed inspiration. She gave it to me as she mouthed the words, "no comment."

"Mr. Davis, I'm afraid I have no comment at this time."

"Does that mean that you will have a comment later?" he asked.

"As I said, I have no comment."

"Mr. Boulder," he continued, "I have already confirmed that you have been hired in this case, so that's not an issue. Could I meet with you and talk to you off the record? I may be able to help you in your investigation."

"And when would you want to do this?" I asked.

"I'll meet you tomorrow at 1:30 p.m. at the Mayflower Café on Capitol Street," he said with finality.

"See you there," I said, as I hung up the telephone.

I related the details of the conversation to Laura. She was immediately skeptical about his motives. I could not disagree with her, and assured her that I would keep my eyes open.

We spent the next three and a half hours solving the world's problems—Jackson, Mississippi's in particular. I cooked up some spaghetti, tossed a salad, and retrieved a bottle of cabernet sauvignon from my modest wine stock. Over dinner, we discussed the upcoming 10:00 p.m. news broadcast. To say that I enjoy Laura's company would be an understatement. She is one of the most intelligent women I have ever met. I knew from high school days that she was smart. I remember the day she verbally annihilated the captain of a visiting debate team during our senior year. She is also a gifted conversationalist. But, beside all of that, she has a way of reading me—of knowing how I feel. She knows that I'm always making mental notes to do things which I never get around to doing. Our relationship was now at a plateau where we saw each other exclusively, and delighted in each other's company. Both of us were satisfied. Marriage was not on the horizon, because neither of us needed it for fulfillment.

As 10:00 p.m. approached, we settled in my living room on the large, cushy sectional sofa. We were prepared for anything. I turned on the tube and switched to Channel 3.

"In tonight's major story, Jackson police are alleged to be negligent in the handling of a rash of kidnappings," said the attractive, black anchorwoman. "Earlier this evening, Timothy Tyler, candidate for mayor, made the allegations."

The TV image switched to the Tyler press conference. It was shown in its entirety. The pretty anchorwoman reappeared.

"Walter Fox, the other mayoral candidate, told us by telephone earlier tonight that his opponent's charge did not stand review, and that it sounded more like grandstanding than genuine concern for the youth of the city.

"WLBT News has also learned that a private investigator has been hired by either the City of Jackson or the Jackson Business Association to try to prove that the police are not involved."

Although Laura and I watched the remainder of the newscast, neither of us could tell you what we saw. I did not relish the idea of this case becoming public, but I also knew that I could handle it. I had been involved in more than one high profile case in my career in St. Louis.

Laura bid me goodnight and departed for her home in Belhaven, a desirable neighborhood a few blocks north of downtown Jackson. Her car had been parked all day in one of my two assigned parking spots at Capitol Place.

Chapter 8

The next morning, I awoke at 7:00 a.m. and headed out on my usual jog to Millsaps College and back. It was going to be another hot day in the capital city. As was customary, I jogged past the Millsaps-Buie House, a grand, multi-story Victorian that had been turned into a bed and breakfast. Many VIP visitors to Jackson stayed there. I had never spent an evening in the place, and resolved to put that on my growing list of things to do when I get a little free time.

As I ran along my route, I thought of the events of last night, and how this case was turning into a circus. A three-ring circus, at that. Timothy Tyler in one ring, Walter B. Fox in another, and yours truly in the third ring. Not to worry, I told myself, it will all be over in a few days. The election was next Tuesday. One candidate would be mayor; the other one would be history. The case of the kidnappings would probably go away. Or would it?

When I returned from my morning run, I was greeted by the blinking red message light on my answering machine. Who would be calling me at this time of day? Probably Laura. I pushed the appropriate button and grabbed a towel for my sweaty face as the device rewound the tape. When it began its playback, the voice that I least expected emanated from it.

"Mr. Boulder, this is Timothy Tyler. I would like to meet with you today. I have some information that might be of value in your investigation. See you at CS's Restaurant on North West Street at 11:45 a.m."

Oh, great. That's all I needed—a meeting with one of the candidates at a busy restaurant at lunchtime. I decided that it would be a great idea to cancel lunch with Timothy Tyler. Besides, I had work to do. I retrieved the telephone book and searched the T's for his telephone number. It was probably unlisted. As I was doing so, the telephone rang. Somewhat startled, I picked it up on the first ring, and answered with a businesslike "hello."

"Good morning, handsome," said Laura. "Care to be seen at lunch having a hot dog in Smith Park with a member of the bar?"

"I would love it," I said. "That beats having lunch with a politician any day." I told her about my message from Tyler, and my decision not to get involved with candidates for mayor. Her reply surprised me.

"Jack, normally I agree with you wholeheartedly, but in this case, I think you should go."

"Why?"

"If you refuse to meet with him, he could imply to the media that you, the investigator hired by the JBA, doesn't want to know the truth—that all you are doing is protecting the police department. And there is another reason," she said, pausing to let her words sink in. "He may actually have evidence of police involvement."

I thought for a few seconds, then said, "He doesn't know that I received the message. If I didn't show up, he would be on thin ice saying that I refused to meet with him."

"That's true," said her words. But the message in her tone was, "what's your point?" I got the message.

"Okay," I said with resignation. "It's hard to argue with a lawyer. Especially one who's right."

We said our good-byes, and I headed for the shower, peeling off my shirt on the way. Before I got across the room, the telephone rang one more time. I figured it was probably Tyler calling again to get me on record about lunch. I picked up the phone and heard the voice of an efficient, middle-aged woman.

"Mr. Boulder. Hold the line please for Mr. Fox."

"This is Walter Fox, Mr. Boulder. I would like to talk with you as soon as possible," he said in a rushed, businesslike manner. "Could you meet me at my office in an hour?"

This must be some sort of dream. Perhaps the events of last evening were causing me to have this vivid hallucination. But I knew otherwise. And I began to have this nagging feeling that the events were beginning to control me, instead of the other way around. I seemed to be in the middle of a stream, on a raft approaching whitewater, unable to get out of the current. I had to ride it out.

"Yes, sir," I replied, instantly wondering why I said "sir."

Chapter 9

Forty-five minutes later, I had showered, shaved, and dressed in my usual polo shirt and khakis. I headed out by foot across Smith Park toward One Jackson Place, twenty stories of gray steel and glass in the heart of downtown Jackson. It is connected by skywalk to Deposit Guaranty Plaza, which is, in turn, connected by skywalk to the Harvey Hotel. It is exactly two blocks from my condo. I caught the elevator up three-fourths of the building to the offices of Fox's law firm. As I exited the elevator, I was immediately greeted by a young receptionist behind a chest-high counter. When I told her I was here to see Walter Fox she escorted me down a hallway to another receptionist, who greeted me in a voice I recognized as that of the caller to my home earlier this morning. This one was about sixty, had white hair, and wore a yellow dress.

"Please come in, and have a seat in Mr. Fox's office. He will be with you in just a few minutes," she said opening the door to an executive office.

His office was furnished in traditional, heavy furniture, and looked down on the green space in front of One Jackson Place. Plaques proclaiming Fox's presidency of this, and support of that, lined the walls. Fox was apparently the first black president of the JBA. There were photographs of him with the President of the United States and the Governor of Mississippi. The outer wall was tinted plate glass from floor to ceiling. As the secretary left the room and closed the door, I walked over to the window and surveyed the scene below. The block that I looked down on had changed more than any other since my days as a youth in Jackson. A contemporary building known as the Landmark Center now stood where the old downtown J.C. Penney store had once been. It took up half the block, including the old sites of Hale and Jones Sporting Goods and WRBC Radio. The only thing left from my high school days on the south side of Capitol Street in that block was the Elite Café, that ever-popular lunch spot known for its yeast rolls and veal cutlets.

In my younger days, the north side of Capitol Street between Lamar and Roach Streets had been home to a number of retail establishments, including the F.W. Woolworth's Store. It received notoriety in the early sixties when some local yokels poured catsup on the heads of some "outside agitators" called freedom riders. Anybody who came to Mississippi during that time period was labeled as an outside agitator. Fortunately, those days were history, and race relations in Mississippi were much improved. As a matter of fact, there were now more black elected officials per capita than in any other state in the country.

Walter B. Fox walked into the room. It was easy to see why he turned heads. He had presence. Standing at six feet, one inch tall, he had close-cropped hair, a neatly trimmed moustache, and a medium black complexion. He wore wire-rimmed glasses, an expensive looking dark blue, pin-striped suit, and a silk maroon tie with white pin dots. His movements were smooth and graceful, as he walked behind the large executive desk, and bid me to sit down in the chair across from him. He rested his elbows on the arms of his chair, and steepled his fingers.

"Thank you for coming on such short notice," he began. "I was wondering if you could give me an update on the progress of your investigation."

"I'm sorry, Mr. Fox. You are not my client. I can only give that information to the one who hired me, unless authorized otherwise."

He swiveled around in his chair, touched a button on the telephone behind him, and pushed a speed-dial button. The telephone speaker broadcasted the ring, and a female voice answered, "Porter Direct Goods. May I help you?"

"This is Walter Fox. Could you put Alvin Porter on the line?"

In less than ten seconds I heard a voice that I recognized as that of the President of the Jackson Business Association.

"Alvin, I have Jack Boulder in my office. Would you assure him that he is authorized to give me a progress report?" said Fox.

"Yes," said Porter. "As a member of the Executive

Committee of the Jackson Business Association, Mr. Fox is entitled to that information."

"Thank you, Alvin," said Fox, as he pushed the button that disconnected the phone line. He turned to me and said, "You may begin."

"As you probably know, I received this assignment about twenty-four hours ago. Therefore, there is not a whole lot to report at this point. I have met with Deputy Chief Dallas, and gotten a good background briefing."

"How long do you think this case will take?" he asked.

"As an attorney, I'm sure you realize the uncertain time element involved in any investigation," I said. "In this case, just about the only way to prove that the police are not doing it, is to prove that someone else is, in fact, doing it. That proof might be very difficult."

"I see," he said, as he picked up a yellow pencil from the top of his desk and began tapping it in the palm of his hand. "I'll be frank with you, Boulder. It is very important to me that this matter not generate a lot of negative publicity about the police department. The JBA supports the police. When I was President of JBA, I pushed for strong support of the police department. If it looks as if it is unworthy of that support, then it is not going to help my campaign."

He got up, and walked over to the window. He put both hands in his pants pockets and gazed outside.

"Boulder," he continued, "I could care less about

being mayor of Jackson. I've got an ideal situation right here. But if Jackson is perceived as having a high crime rate, it is not good for anybody's business, especially downtown businesses. So I plan on doing something about it. I'm willing to give up four years of a good corporate law practice to bring crime under control. I don't care what it takes—more prisons, more cops, whatever. We have got to do this."

"I understand," I said.

"Do you?" he said, turning around to stare at me. His eyes focused in on me like a zoom lens. "Do you, really? Do you know what crime does to business? There is the economic loss, obviously. Then there is the extra money for security. But what is worse is when a business owner sees other businesses moving out. Does he stay longer, or does he pack it in now and head for Ridgeland or Brandon or Clinton? Is it going to get better? The mayor saying it does not make it so. There must be results. Are you aware that security companies have taken to advertising Jackson's national crime rankings on billboards? Just take a ride around town and take a look. It might surprise you that most businesses in Jackson want to stay in Jackson. Crime, Boulder, is a cancer that must be stopped."

"How do you plan to stop crime?" I asked.

"I'll give you a copy of my ten-point plan on your way out, so that you can see the details."

"I thought the crime rate was going down in Jackson," I said.

"Yes, it is," he said. "And we know why, don't we? Juvenile criminals are disappearing."

"Shouldn't that make you happy?" I asked.

"To tell you the truth, it does not bother me a bit. But if it's the police that are taking them, there will be a loss of confidence in law enforcement—even a fear of police. No, as much as I like the idea of the crime rate going down, I like totalitarianism even less. Actually, I think the new jail space has a lot to do with the crime rate going down. Take the worst ten percent of the criminals off the street and watch what happens."

The telephone made a buzzing sound, and the voice of the efficient secretary said, "Mr. Fox, Dennis Davis with WLBT News and his cameraman are here to see you."

I told Fox that I would find my way out. I hoped that Davis would not be bringing the camera person to his 1:30 p.m. meeting with me.

Chapter 10

CS's Restaurant is the kind of place that has an eclectic mixture of patrons, usually including several young lawyers, a state elected official, a few college professors, a group of women, and a construction crew working on a nearby project. The daily lunch special is posted on blackboards on the walls. Poster boards in strategic wall locations announce permanent menu items, such as the Suzie burger, the Inez burger and the Joe B. burger. I'm not even sure if they have a regular menu. There are two rooms for diners. One is a large, open space toward the front door; the other room is smaller and darker, with a pool table, video games and a large screen television. The partition between the rooms is only waist high, giving a feeling of openness. Around the top of the rooms, like crown molding in a fine, old

home, are three shelves of beer cans and beer bottles. There must be over a thousand of them. "Ski Mississippi" tee shirts are available at the counter.

What makes CS's so unique is its display of bumper stickers, some political and some whimsical. Some examples are: "As A Matter of Fact, I Do Own The Road," "Your Mother Is Ugly And She Dresses You Funny," and "I Don't Belong to Any Organized Political Party, I'm A Democrat." Then there is "Remember What Pete Collins Said." Pat, the proprietor, is always glad to tell the curious about Pete Collins.

I parked my Camaro on the side street, walked inside, and scanned the patrons. The place was almost full. Timothy Tyler was sitting at the corner table in the main dining room, right beside the "I Hate Bumper Stickers" bumper sticker, both elbows on the table and arms folded. I thought it odd that none of the patrons paid him any attention. After all, he was a candidate for mayor. He wore chinos and a blue denim work shirt with sleeves rolled up to the elbows. He looked just like he did on television, his distinguishing characteristics being dark, red hair and a thick, red moustache. I waded through the pond of chairs and tables and walked over to him. He remained seated, and looked me right in the eye.

"Mr. Tyler?" I asked.

Remaining seated, he stuck out his right hand and said, "That's right. You must be Mr. Boulder."

I shook his hand and sat down. A waitress immediately appeared and took our orders for the meat loaf special. The man who wanted to be mayor spoke first.

"I'm going to speak very bluntly with you, Mr. Boulder," he said firmly. "Did you see my statement on the news last night?"

"I did."

"Then you know my position. I think the police are kidnapping those kids."

"Why would they do that?" I asked.

"Look, you know as well as I do that crime has gotten out of hand in Jackson. We have a generation of kids who have been neglected by the system, and who only know the ways of the street. One of these days, we are going to wake up and realize that we just can't go on letting poor, teenage girls have babies and not expect any consequences. Do you know that we now have schools where students are bringing their children to school? And you know what else we won't face up to?" He raised his right index finger but kept it pointing towards the ceiling. "Many of these girls are pregnant by their stepfathers, cousins, mothers' boyfriends, and who knows who else. We blame the girls, but many times it's outright rape. It is time for intervention, and prevention."

"I couldn't agree with you more," I said.

"I understand the pressure that the police are under. But I have information that a rogue group of cops are responsible for this."

"Would you care to share that information?"

"I can tell you who I got it from," he said. "I just hope that he will talk to you. He is a decent person who cares about the community."

"What's his name?'

"Jeremiah Travis," said Tyler. "He runs a halfway house for prisoners who are on work release. He knows everything there is to know about what's going on in the 'hood."

Our lunches arrived, and we began eating. A woman in her late twenties, wearing a long, print dress and sandals, came over and approached Tyler. "Excuse me for interrupting, but I just wanted to shake your hand and wish you good luck. It was a courageous thing you did yesterday, and I want you to know that you have my vote."

Tyler thanked her softly, and she turned and left with a group of women similar in age.

"Why do you want to be mayor?" I asked, surprised at the question as it came from my lips.

"Can't you see why?"

"No."

"It is obvious that the establishment has given up and moved to the suburbs. There are not many who care anymore. Mr. Boulder, we are at a crossroads, and something has to be done, and done now. We can't survive another generation."

"Then why are you so concerned about these thugs who are missing?" I asked, my voice rising. "All of them have rap sheets. Even if they were found, they would all be arrested because there are outstanding warrants on every single one of them."

"Are you kidding me?" he asked, his tone indicating that this was the first time he had heard this news.

"Not one bit," I said.

"That still doesn't make a difference. No one has the right to kidnap them. Especially the police."

"But you don't know it's the police," I pointed out.

"After you talk to Jeremiah, you will feel the same way that I do," he said. He reached in his shirt pocket, laid a business card on the table, and said, "Here is his telephone number. He's expecting you to call."

Over small talk we finished our meals, then walked up to the counter and told the proprietor what we had for lunch. This was one place where the honor system was still in effect. He paid for his meal, and I paid for mine. For that I was glad. I don't know if I would have had the *chutzpah* to put a meal for Timothy Tyler on my expense report to the JBA.

There was something about Tyler that left me a bit unsettled. He was not what I thought he was going to be. There was a gentleness and sincerity about him that was genuine. What he had expressed told me that he was informed about the social strata at the poverty level, and below. As a police officer, I had been on many calls where I got an up close and personal look at what family life was really like in the urban inner city. Even though he was branded a liberal, his thoughts on some of the social ills did not sound liberal. He might make a good mayor.

Chapter 11

A summer thundershower found its way to CS's as I opened the door to the Camaro. This was not good. The Camaro had been restored to its original condition, and its 1968 sticker did not show air-conditioning as one of its options. As a matter of fact, it was equipped only with an AM radio, four-speed transmission, tinted windows, and a heater. Under the hood was a 327-cubic-inch engine that produced over 200 horsepower. All of this perched on a set of Tiger Paws. It was a car that was meant to get from Point A to Point B in minimum time, and it did that very well indeed. Unfortunately, it was a dangerous car in the rain because most of the car's weight rested on the front end. The rear end was prone to slip sideways at the least bit of acceleration on a wet road.

I took the so-called inner city route downtown, instead of the faster and busier West Street. I wanted to go slow, and ride through a neighborhood where drug pushers might be on corners. Not that I wanted to interview them, you understand. I could imagine the response if I pulled up to a group on a street corner, and asked if they knew anything about the missing dealers. They would not hesitate to tell me where I could take my Camaro. Actually, they would probably just take my Camaro, and tell me where I go. I merely wanted to observe.

I turned left on Lamar Street and considered the boarded-up houses on either side of the street. Such a shame. The rain came down harder, and my windshield began fogging up. Another disadvantage of not having air-conditioning. Perhaps I should reconsider and have a unit installed. I made a mental note to look into the feasibility of doing just that. The rain was coming down harder now, and the windshield was getting foggier. Visibility was down to about fifty feet through the front windshield. I pulled into the parking lot of a convenience store and removed the cellular telephone that I kept in the glove compartment. I plugged it in the cigarette lighter outlet and dialed the number that Tyler had given me for Jeremiah Travis. Someone answered on the first ring.

"Christ Is The Answer," said the voice of a male in his early twenties.

I asked to speak to Jeremiah Travis. He was on the phone in a few seconds. I told him who I was, and that Timothy Tyler had recommended that I give him a call.

"I can meet you at the Subway Lounge on West Pearl at 4:00," he said with authority.

"I'll be there," I replied.

I drove back to Capitol Place, and parked the car in its assigned place. The rain was beginning to let up. I had ten minutes before my 1:30 p.m. appointment with Dennis Davis at the Mayflower. I decided to walk, since it was only three blocks through the heart of downtown. Ten minutes later, wet with perspiration from the humidity and muggy air, I walked under an art deco canopy and into one of Jackson's oldest continuously operating restaurants. "Since 1935" proclaims the sign in the front window. The café was one big room, booths along most of the walls, tables in the middle and a genuine lunch counter on the left side. The floor was a carpet of small, black and white octagonal tiles. The walls displayed mounted fish, framed photographs of Jackson scenes, and various icons of the sea. It was a seafood place. On the menu were four varieties of redfish. And that wasn't counting "THE ACROPOLIS SPECIAL," which was described on the menu as "Broiled redfish with sautéed crabmeat, garnished with shrimp and oysters, and served with our special seafood sauce." My personal favorite menu item was the Mayflower Greek Salad—"fresh lump crabmeat on a bed of lettuce with feta cheese, calmata olives and pepperoni peppers."

Like a hawk that patiently waits atop a Mississippi roadside telephone pole for an unsuspecting field mouse to enter its field of view, Dennis Davis sat erect in a booth on the right, near the rear of the café. His chin rested on clasped hands, elbows on the top of the table. Judging from the full head of salt and pepper hair, I guessed him to be in his mid-forties. He wore a fashionable blue dress shirt with white collar, a yellow pinpoint necktie and gold-rimmed glasses. Somehow I knew that the eyeglasses would be bifocals, and confirmed that fact as I approached to within a few feet of him. He remained seated and stuck out his right hand.

"Mr. Boulder, I presume," he said, in the deep voice of one who has spent many years behind a microphone. I shook his hand as I sat down on the other side of the booth, my back toward the front door. At that instant, I heard a sharp noise on the top of the table and looked down to see a salt shaker laying on its side. Davis reached down, picked it up with his right hand, and poured a generous amount of its contents in a little pile. He then took the shaker and set it down on its bottom edge so that the glass object was leaning at a forty-five degree angle. With both hands he carefully balanced the shaker and then removed his hands, moving them to a position up and in front of him in the "I give up" position. His head leaned forward and downward to the side of the container, which was now balanced on the small pile of salt. He formed an "O" with his lips and carefully blew most of the salt away, leaving the shaker resting precariously on what could be only one or two grains of salt. As he exhaled, I detected stale breath characteristic of a heavy smoker. He leaned back, lowered his hands to his lap, and looked me straight in the eye. I took only three seconds of his stare before looking back down at the leaning salt shaker.

"That's a pretty good trick," I remarked casually.

He laughed, tapped the table lightly with his left

hand, causing the salt shaker to fall, and said with a grin, "Kids are fascinated by it. You ought to see the little ones in a family restaurant when I do it."

"How did you discover such a trick of physics?" I asked.

"My uncle was a truck driver. I used to ride with him when I was a kid. He would pull that big, eighteen-wheeler into a truck stop, then do that little trick in the café on the top of the table. Other truckers could never duplicate it. It's simply a matter of balance and a flat surface. The funny thing about it is that once you do it the first time, it's easy as pie."

The waiter, an older man who wore a heavily starched, gray waiter's coat, took our order for coffee and had two cups sitting in front of us faster than a meter maid could write a parking ticket. Davis poured a stream of sugar in his coffee; then added the full measure of a shot of pre-packaged, liquid creamer. I left my coffee black, and studied the framed photo on the wall above our table while Davis performed his ritual. The black and white photograph was dated November 9, 1928, and depicted the terminal building at Hawkins Field, currently a general aviation industrial park in northwest Jackson. The inscription read, "Dedication of Jackson Airport."

"I understand you just moved to Jackson," he said, stirring the concoction in the heavy white cup.

"About six months ago."

"Where from?" he asked.

"St. Louis. I retired from my job there, and came back to where I grew up."

"Wait a minute!" he said excitedly as he snapped his fingers. "Jack Boulder. Jack Boulder! Yeah, you're the cop who shot the guy who shot your partner. Wrote that getting-even book. Yeah," he said as realization was dawning on him. "I've got your book. It's pretty good, too. Ways to get even." He stuck his hand across the table. "It's a pleasure to meet you, Jack Boulder."

"Likewise," I said drily.

"Listen, maybe we could do a story on you one day? The detective who came home from the cold."

"I don't know if there would be much interest in that," I said, sipping my coffee. "You were going to tell me about a lead that you were going to share with me?" I said, making the sentence a question.

"Right," he said, pausing to gather his thoughts. "We have been hearing for a long time that there are two cops who work in the west central Jackson precinct who are known to take some of the bad guys to the end of the road, if you know what I mean."

"I am afraid that I don't."

"Our sources tell us that when certain known local criminals beat a rap, they are visited by these two cops, and then, strangely, are never seen again."

"Have there ever been any missing person reports filed in such cases?" I asked.

"None that we know of. But usually the guys who disappear are so mean that even their families are happy to see them go."

"Any evidence of foul play?"

"No."

"So, based on that, you think these two officers are involved in this case?"

"We are told that they are openly taking credit for helping the crime rate go down," he said.

"Care to tell me who they might be?"

"Would you care to give us an exclusive interview if you prove it's them?"

"No can do," I answered. "The results of my investigation belong to my client."

"Which happens to be the JBA?" he asked with a grin.

I didn't answer. Instead, I picked up my cup and had another sip of coffee. I held the brew to my lips and focused on a spot right between his eyes.

"Okay, you win," he finally said. "But promise me that if you talk to any media that you will talk to WLBT first."

"I'll make that promise," I said.

Leaning forward, he lowered his voice and said, "The two cops are Lamar Workman and George McNair. They ride together. And they are bad dudes. I hear that all they do on their days off is work out at the police academy gymnasium. You can't miss them.

They both look like overgrown bodybuilders. They always work the midnight shift."

"I appreciate the lead. I'll see what I can find out."

"And you will call me before you call any other media?" he said with raised eyebrows and a smile.

I excused myself and slid out of the seat, leaving him to return to his salt shaker. At the cash register, I laid a five dollar bill on the glass countertop as our waiter scurried to the front of the café. As he made change, a large, color photograph on a wall near the front window caught my eye. In the photo were a young boy sitting at a lunch counter, a uniformed police officer sitting beside him, and a soda jerk behind the counter. The youngster was obviously the center of attention. Beside the large photo was a framed eight-by-ten copy of a Norman Rockwell front cover of a *Saturday Evening Post*. It was one of the magazine's most famous covers. Then I noticed it.

"Hey," I said to the man behind the register. "That's you in the picture, isn't it?"

He swelled with pride and confirmed that it was.

"We love police officers and kids," he said with a Greek-laden accent.

"Me, too," I said. "Keep the change."

I walked out the front door and headed up Capitol Street toward my home and office. Going "up" Capitol Street means heading east up a slight hill toward the Old State Capitol, which served as the seat of Mississippi government until 1903. It now presents the state's past in its role as the State Historical Museum.

After crossing Lamar Street, I took a left, walked inside the mall at Deposit Guaranty Plaza, and was immediately greeted by the aroma of freshly brewed coffee from a coffee bar. The bouquet of coffee beans competed with the smell of freshly popped popcorn from the ever-present, and ever-popular, popcorn wagon that is domiciled in the mall foyer. I succumbed to the coffee aroma, sauntered over, and ordered a cup of Kona. I took a seat at one of the small wrought-iron tables in front of the coffee bar. At the adjacent table were two men in their middle twenties, wearing white shirts and neckties. I suspected that they were on break from their lower-to-middle management jobs somewhere in this very building. I couldn't help overhearing their conversation.

"I don't give a damn if the police are kidnapping the little bastards or not," said the first voice.

"Listen," said voice number two. "I've got a buddy on the department who says that when the numbers come out next week, overall crime will be down almost fifty percent."

"Outstanding. It's about time for a little payback."

I didn't listen to the rest of their conversation. I knew where it was going. Which was more than I could say for my investigation. I could not tell which way it was headed. It was almost 3:30 p.m. Time for me to get in my car and head to The Subway Lounge and the Summers Hotel. I walked back to Capitol Place. Perhaps it was due to cleansing of the air by the rain, or maybe it was the caffeine, but I felt a slight spring in my step. The air was cleaner. Things were fresher. It is funny how such feelings come upon one. I hoped that it was a foreshadowing of good things to come.

Chapter 12

I retrieved the Camaro from its parking spot at Capitol Place and drove to 619 West Pearl Street, the location of The Subway Lounge. It was in the basement of a two-story, dark red brick building upon which hung a sign proclaiming "Hotel Summers." The building and the neighborhood both looked like they had seen better days. Next to the hotel was a graveled, vacant lot, then a couple of houses that looked occupied, and then a congregation of tenement houses that looked as if they each couldn't have contained more than six-hundred square feet of living area.

I parked the car in the vacant lot and went inside The Subway, stepping down into the lounge. A handwritten sign on the door declared "Cover Charge $5." I allowed a few seconds for my eyes to adjust to the dim lights. What little light that was in the joint was made up of brilliant colors from neon beer signs on the wall and behind the bar. Two black men who appeared to be in their late fifties or early sixties came into focus. One was standing behind the bar in the stance of a bartender, while the other played the role of customer, sitting on a barstool. The bartender wore a black T-shirt that had the word "JAZZ" emblazoned on the front in large white letters. The customer wore dark pants, a white shirt, and a checkered jacket. I walked across the room and said, "Good afternoon." Neither man replied, choosing instead just to stare at me. I walked over and stood beside the customer on the barstool, and said, "I'm supposed to meet Jeremiah Travis here at four."

"You just met him," said the one on the barstool. "Let's sit down at this table over here."

"Is this place open yet?" I asked.

"Oh no," he replied. "The Subway is a late night place. It doesn't really get going until after midnight. How about something cold to drink?"

"Sure," I said.

He turned to the bartender, and said, "Sam, bring us two cold ones."

"Coming right up," said the man behind the bar, turning around and reaching downward. Within seconds, two bottles of cola were resting on the small, round table in front of us. The bartender seemed in no hurry to leave, so I gave him two dollars. He returned to his station behind the bar. Travis took a swig from his bottle of soft drink and patiently waited for me to speak.

"Timothy Tyler seems to think a lot of you," I said.

"It's mutual," he countered, without changing expression.

"I'll get right to the point. I'm conducting an investigation into the missing young men. He thinks you may be able to help."

"It's possible," he said thoughtfully. "I can point you in a direction. I believe it to be the right one. But it's a road you will not be able to travel unless you have connections with people who understand the gang situation in Jackson. Do you have such a connection?"

"I do," I said. It was sort of true, if one counts my contacts at the police department.

"There are two main gangs. One is The Blues; the other is The Greens. The Blues used to call themselves The Souls, and the Greens were known as The Vipers. The Jackson Police Department has been getting better this past year at slowing down the drug dealing. Many of the bigger dealers are now at the State Penitentiary at Parchman or at the Hinds County Penal Farm. What I'm saying is that the market has had pressure on it." He took a swig that emptied half his cola bottle and continued. "The Blues decided they needed to wipe out The Greens, so they started getting their guys. At first, they just ran them out of town. But lately, I understand that they have taken to doing worse things. Of course, The Greens have retaliated. Nobody knows how long it's gonna go on, but it will get worse before it gets better. Soon, there will be innocent people—kids, mostly— who will get in the way. It needs to be stopped, now."

"Do you have any specifics?" I asked.

"It's common knowledge. If you spent any time in this community, you would know it, too."

His implication was clear. I decided it was time to change the subject.

"How long has the Summers Hotel been in operation?" I asked. "I didn't even know it was here."

"Did you grow up in Jackson?"

"I did."

"Did you know what it was like during segregation?"

"What do you mean?"

"Until the laws were changed, Jackson was a totally segregated town. Black folks had their own city within the city. They even had their own Chamber of Commerce. Farish Street was the center of it all. You ever heard of the Crystal Palace?"

I shook my head from side to side.

"How 'bout the Blackstone Café?"

"Sorry. But I don't think I was old enough then. I was born in 1950."

"Well, let me tell you the way it was."

I crossed my legs and took a sip from the bottle in front of me. Jeremiah Travis leaned forward and began talking. As he did so, the bartender came around from behind the bar, and sat down at our table. I had a feeling this was going to take awhile.

"A man by the name of Bill Summers opened this hotel around 1943. He owned the Blackstone Café, which was where the McCoy Federal Building, on Farish and Capitol, now sits. He was also a promoter of black bands, dances and the like. White people were always coming into the café with their chauffeurs, maids and cooks. The whites had hotels to stay in, but their servants had to be farmed out to black families in town. That's how this hotel came into being. Bill

Summers bought this place from a white man—it was a rooming house—and started one of the first hotels for blacks in Jackson. This place is a landmark."

"Did any famous blacks ever stay here?"

"Are you kidding? Lots of famous black artists came to Jackson in those days, and most of them stayed right here. When Nat King Cole stayed here, this place was inundated with fans, both black and white. The whites couldn't attend his concert, but they could come to the hotel and see him. Mr. and Mrs. Summers allowed the white folks the privilege of coming into the lobby to get his autograph. And Nat King Cole wasn't the only one. Duke Ellington, 'Dizzy' Gillespie, Count Basie, and Lionel Hampton have all spent the night here in the hotel. They would play at the Crystal Palace Ballroom on Farish Street, and then stay here. It was quite a time."

He went on for more than twenty minutes, reminiscing about the great and not-so-great jazz and blues artists who stayed at the 40-room hotel. Finally, he brought himself back to the present, as quickly as he had reverted to the past. I could have listened as long as he would talk. This was a part of Jackson's history that I knew nothing about. But he had finished. And I needed additional information.

"One more thing," I said. "What do you know about a couple of cops named Workman and McNair?"

He erupted with a belly laugh, as did his friend the

bartender. "You mean Pete and Repeat. They look bad, and they play the part to the hilt. But they are good guys. They keep peace when others can't."

"Could they have anything to do with the missing dealers?"

"Not a chance," he said. "You go check out the Blues and the Greens. That's where you're gonna find your kidnappers."

I thanked them and left the Summers Hotel and The Subway Lounge. My mood was now a mixture of melancholy and enthusiasm. I was making some progress on the case, but I still had a long way to go. I needed a break, and I needed it fast.

WEDNESDAY

Chapter 13

During my morning jog up North State Street, I began to mentally sort out the coming day and reflect on what I had learned so far about this case. There was no doubt that someone or some group was removing many of Jackson's street corner drug dealers from their normal habitat. Just to be scientific and identify all of the possible alternatives, I considered the possibility that all of the so-called victims had removed themselves. Perhaps they had gone off together to the annual National Convention of Drug Dealers. A scenario such as that was so unlikely, I immediately laughed it off. The logical suspects, then, were an unidentified group of police officers, Officers Pete and Repeat, a single police officer, The Blues, The Greens, or some other unknown individual or group. I had too many suspects, and too little time. The election was only a few days away.

As I bounced my way up State Street, my mood turned melancholy, just like yesterday at The Subway. Jackson had missed many opportunities. One of those was the preservation of houses on North State Street. Jogging past the white-columned Fagan House on my left, it was easy to imagine what it must have been like. The Fagan House was a two-story treasure that has been home to many a wedding reception.

Past the Fagan House is a two-block commercial strip consisting of buildings that have no relation to each other at all. An urban planner would be sick at the sight of self-service gasoline stations juxtaposing three generations of medical buildings. A fast food restaurant now stands on the site of one of Jackson's favorite former meeting and dining places—Primos Restaurant. It was destroyed by fire in the early nineties.

I glided down the hill in front of the Mississippi Baptist Medical Center, then started up an incline alongside the Beth Israel cemetery. This was the steepest part of my jogging route, but the most beautiful. Here in the seven-hundred block of North State Street were five big, beautiful houses in a row. Now this was the way I imagined the street to have been. Fairview Street, which runs east off State Street, just before Millsaps College, is where the Warren-Guild-Simmons House, better known these days as the Fairview Inn, can be found. It, and the Millsaps-Buie House are clearly the two finest bed and breakfast inns in Jackson. Fairview Inn was built in 1908, and was designed by the Chicago architectural firm of Spencer and Powers. As a B & B it is one of the best-kept secrets in Jackson because so many Jacksonians are not aware of its availability and its amenities. I made a mental note to spend a weekend in this epitome of a southern mansion this autumn.

I made my U-turn in front of Millsaps College and

took my time getting back to Capitol Place, stopping in at Frank's World Famous Biscuits on North President Street to pick up a couple of biscuits with sausage. I showered, made some fresh dark roast coffee, poured myself a tall glass of orange juice, and opened the French doors to the balcony. I took a seat at the table and gazed at the surroundings. The view up and to my left was the clock tower of the Lamar Life Building, with its Roman numerals and gargoyles. The American flag fluttered gently in the early morning breeze. Across the street the mockingbirds were especially playful as they chased each other around the tops of the magnolias, redbuds, dogwoods and oaks of Smith Park. Through the trees of the park, I could see the gold cross atop St. Peter's Cathedral. Every Sunday morning at precisely 10:30 a.m. the sound of bells could be heard from that direction. It doesn't take long to learn the rhythms of the city. I glanced to the right and bid a good morning to Gertrude, standing proudly with wings spread, on top of the Capitol.

What was it like in this very spot on June 3, 1903, the anniversary of the birthday of Jefferson Davis and the day that the "New" Capitol was dedicated? In a sense, I felt like I knew what it had been like. My grandfather Benjamin Franklin Sullivan had been here, and he had described it in great detail to me when I was a little boy. The crowd, according to the daily newspaper, was between 20,000 and 25,000. Grandpa Sullivan said it was 30,000. The streets were decorated with banners and ribbons, and a big parade was held from downtown to the New Capitol. Governor Longino led the parade, followed by government officials, the United Daughters of the Confederacy and a contingent of weathered Confederate veterans carrying their tattered and torn battle flags. I could imagine them passing me by on Congress Street, with crowds four-deep along the side of the street.

When the crowd got to the Capitol, the cornerstone was laid by the Grand Officers of the Grand Lodge of the Masons. Two hours of speeches by the Governor, the Chief Justice and Bishop Charles B. Galloway were interrupted by a summer thunderstorm, causing the crowd to move inside. Grandpa said that on that day, he was the proudest he had ever been in his life. As a matter of fact, he was so proud of being a Jacksonian that he decided right then and there to name his firstborn son after Andrew Jackson, the city's namesake. He never got a chance to carry out that wish, however, because his only child was a girl. At the age of twenty-one, my mother married John Boulder, and nine months after their wedding day, I was born. They honored Grandpa Sullivan's request and named me Andrew Jackson Boulder. With such a pedigree, I should have known that I was destined to return to Jackson.

My thoughts returned to the present and the mayor's race. People these days talk about how ugly politics has become. They should read a little history and study Andrew Jackson's presidential race. But that's another story.

The telephone sounded and I picked it up immediately. It was Laura.

"Good morning," she said with a spring in her voice. "How was your run this morning?"

"The run was good, but I kept thinking about the old houses on State Street."

"I know what you mean," she said as if she had something on her mind. "I'm calling to ask you to lunch."

"I'd love it, of course," I said with a smile. "Where to?"

"My civic club."

"That doesn't mean I have to get out the necktie, does it?"

"I'm afraid so," she said.

"What's on the program?"

"You are going to be interested in this one," she said. "The two candidates for mayor are going to speak."

Chapter 14

The Downtown Club met in the ballroom of the Harvey Hotel. Average attendance was in the three hundred range. It had its genesis in World War II at the Heidelberg Hotel on Capitol Street. Originally, its purpose was to link the officer corps at the Jackson Air Base at Hawkins Field with the Jackson business community. Every Wednesday, there would be a speaker or program, and the officers, many of whom were pilots from other parts of the world, would come downtown to join the locals. Jackson, unlike many other cities, had a reputation as a good host for military personnel. And every Wednesday since then, the club has met downtown.

At 11:50 a.m., I walked over to the Harvey and found Laura waiting for me in the mezzanine lobby. I wore my only necktie, a red and blue striped silk model, gray slacks, and a blue blazer. Laura looked professional and attractive in a red suit and navy scarf. We greeted each other without embracing, then found a table in the middle of the room. We then made our way through a buffet line featuring entrées of fried catfish, lasagna and roast beef. Buffet lines are much more efficient, since the program is limited to one hour, and there are three hundred mouths to feed. We ate quickly and shared small talk with the other six people at our table. There were five men and one woman seated at the head table.

I recognized only two of them. Timothy Tyler sat at the far left, and Walter B. Fox at the far right. I wondered if that was a Freudian slip.

A bell on the head table rang, and a middle-aged man in a dark blue suit rose to a position behind the podium, asking us all to stand and say the pledge of allegiance. We complied faithfully. The food that we had already eaten was then blessed by the pastor of a local church.

"We would now like to recognize our guests," said the man behind the podium.

He pointed to his left at a table about midway in the room. A man stood up and said that he would like to introduce Bob Stevens, ". . . who is in the insurance business." Suddenly almost three hundred strong voices enthusiastically said in unison, "Welcome, Bob!" This continued several more times, until, to my horror, Laura stood up. I couldn't believe it. Was she really going to do it? How could I stop it? I felt that my disguise in an undercover case was about to be blown, and there was nothing I could do about it. I also knew that Fox and Tyler would soon be pointing their fingers at me, literally. Panic was about to overtake any remaining semblance of control. Laura was going to regret this.

"I'd like the club to meet Darryl Simeon, a new associate in our law firm," she said, gesturing to a young man of about twenty-five across the table from me. She immediately sat down.

"Welcome, Darryl!" came the loud refrain.

I felt a hand on my forearm and looked at Laura, who was staring at me.

Leaning forward, she whispered, "Are you alright?"

Composing myself, I said, "Just fine, thank you."

After introduction of the guests, there came a brief business report, and the introduction of the speakers. The man behind the podium, whom I had now deduced to be the president of the club, said that the order of speeches by the mayoral candidates had been determined earlier by coin toss, and that Walter B. Fox would be first. A man sitting to the left of the podium was called to make the introduction. He rose to the podium.

"Ladies and gentlemen of the Downtown Club, our city faces a crisis. But there is one good thing about a crisis. From it emerges a person who can take command and steer our city through it. It is my honor to ask you to please welcome Jackson's next mayor, our own Walter Fox."

There was an immediate standing ovation. I leaned to Laura, and remarked, "Looks like this group likes Mr. Fox."

"They should," she replied. "He was president of the club last year."

When the applause died down, Fox took his position, planted his feet shoulder-width apart and stood erectly. He wore a black suit, white shirt and red tie. He looked the part.

"How many of you have been a victim of crime during the past twelve months, or know someone who has?" he began.

A hand went up from almost every person in the room. As I surveyed the room, I noticed three television cameras at the rear, along with what appeared to be several reporters taking notes. I turned back toward the speaker.

"Crime is a cancer and it must be stopped, or it will spread, and eventually kill the host. We have a cancer growing in Jackson, and it must be stopped before it grows any further. It is a sad state of affairs when alarm companies and developers mention crime on billboard advertising."

He went on for about ten minutes on the theme of family values and the general moral decline of society. It seemed rather monotone, as if he had said it a hundred times or more. It was without passion. Then he paused, became more animated, and released his parting shot at this most friendly audience.

"I have a plan to do something about crime in Jackson. You can pick up a copy at the back of the room on your way out. Number one on that plan is to build more jails, especially juvenile detention centers. There has been some talk lately about the crime rate going down. Have you noticed that crime seemed to decline as soon as more jail space became available?"

There was applause. He continued.

"There is another factor that is contributing to crime going down in Jackson. Our police department is doing a better job—a smarter job." His voice grew louder. "And we don't need to abandon them now!" Lots of applause. "Finally, let me address one of the most ridiculous charges ever made in a political campaign. My opponent has made libelous, unfounded allegations that the police are kidnapping drug dealers in this town. Is that not the silliest thing you have ever heard?" He paused and smiled. "Let me make it clear. I would never condone such behavior. But have you noticed that our society seems to be a little better off these past few weeks, with so many drug dealers off the streets? This is a great city, with a great past and a great future. Let's keep it that way. No. Let's make it better. And you can help do that by voting for Walter Fox next Tuesday. Thank you."

Another standing ovation. I felt sorry for Timothy Tyler. It would be no fun to follow an act like that. Fox sat down, and the president of the club returned to the podium and said, "And now, our next candidate, Timothy Tyler."

There was polite applause as Tyler stepped to the podium. He wore a blue blazer, gray slacks and a multi-colored necktie. He was somewhat soft-spoken and matter-of-fact as he began to make his remarks.

"One of the things that is tough about running for mayor is that one has to run against such an eloquent speaker as my opponent—a man who has been educated at the finest schools, and has had the best post-college educational opportunities that the state's largest law firm can buy. My speaking experience has been limited to neighborhood organizations and community groups. And that is why I think my opponent has his eyes closed to reality when it comes to crime. I, also, am an advocate of public safety and reduced crime. A strong advocate. But I am also a realist. Let me tell you a story. A story that is true. When I attended high school in the public schools of Jackson, a girl in my class became pregnant. Now, just for the record, I didn't have anything to do with it." There was pleasant laughter. "I believe her name was Linda. When she started showing, she left school and went to a place they called a home for unwed mothers." There were nods throughout the audience. "I have never seen Linda again. I hope she is doing well. That was thirty years ago. Today, we have middle schools—grades six, seven and eight—where students bring THEIR children to school."

It was obvious that this audience was now connected with Tyler. Every eye was on him, rapt in attention.

"Ladies and gentlemen, we need to pay more attention to the prevention of crime. We must somehow intercede in the lives of these young, teenage girls who are getting pregnant. Some of you will be quick to blame the young girls. But before you do, ask about the fathers. And what you will find is that the fathers of those children are not the hormone-charged boyfriends of those girls. Many times, the baby's father is a cousin, an uncle or a stepfather. Or even the boyfriend of the girl's mother. Our society has indeed changed dramatically over the past thirty years. But, what will the future hold if we don't do something about education and prevention now?

"I would like to close with a story that I believe illustrates the situation. It is about two men who are out fishing in the middle of a river. Suddenly, a baby, struggling in the current, drifts by. One of the men reaches out and rescues the baby. Then another baby comes by, and the other fisherman reaches out for it. Soon there are more babies. One fisherman jumps out of the boat, swims to the bank and starts to run upstream. His fishing partner demands to know why he is abandoning the job of rescuing the babies. The fisherman replies, 'I'm going upstream to stop someone from throwing those babies in the water.' "

Tyler stood silently for no more than six seconds, but it seemed like six minutes. Body still, his eyes scanned the audience like the rotating beacon of a lighthouse. Then he turned, went back to his chair and sat down. There was silence, then one pair of hands applauded, then a few more. Suddenly, there was strong, sustained applause. He did not receive a standing ovation. But he had connected with the Downtown Club. That fact was borne out, as the meeting adjourned and the crowd filed out. More than once I heard the comment, "You know, Tyler made a good point."

As we were making our way through the crowd Laura softly said in my ear, "Did you notice that Tyler never said a word about the kidnappings?"

All I could say was "Hmm."

As we passed through the large wooden doors of the convention hall, a bright light hit my eyes and I saw a pinholed, silver microphone bearing the letters and logo of WLBT thrust up to my chin. I heard the deep voice of Dennis Davis ask, "Excuse me sir, would you give me your reaction to the speeches you just heard?"

My body went numb and I could not think. Somehow I heard myself say, "In my opinion, both candidates did an excellent job of stating their positions and beliefs."

THURSDAY

Chapter 15

Detail work needed to be done. So I spent the day interviewing several police officers who had taken missing person reports, reviewing numerous files at the police department, and riding around, getting to know the neighborhoods that were the subject of the investigation. Thursday evening, I watched the 10:00 news, hoping to learn something more. After the news, I reclined on my sofa and thought of all the possibilities involved. There were too many.

My thoughts were interrupted by the telephone making its electronic warble. It was Deputy Chief Dallas.

"Care to go cruise the 'hood?"

I told him it would take me five minutes to get ready.

Ten minutes later, a dark green Lexus two-door coupe pulled alongside the yellow painted curb in front of Capitol Place. Its windows were tinted darker than normal, but not so dark that I didn't recognize the face of the driver, Deputy Chief Tom Dallas. I scooted around the vehicle, opened the passenger door, and sat down in the finest leather seat I've ever had the pleasure of meeting. There's nothing like the smell of leather in a car.

"Nice patrol car," I said with a grin.

He told me that it was among the fruits of a recent

drug bust, and that it had been forfeited. Now it could be used against the bad guys. I noticed a portable blue light sitting on the console, its power cord halfway in the cigarette lighter. Beside it was a cellular telephone, its numbers casting a lime green glow.

Dallas was dressed in a black tee shirt with black combat fatigue pants. I couldn't see underneath the dash, but I bet he was wearing combat boots. I guess the style would be called "SWAT team casual." In his lap was a walkie-talkie that made little robotic sounds between transmissions.

We headed south on Congress Street, then took a right on Pearl, a straight shot into the west central part of the city. As we drove past the old, abandoned King Edward Hotel, I thought of what this block must have been like fifty years ago, when railroads were in their heyday and the commercial center of Jackson was Capitol and Mill Streets, with the King Edward located diagonally across from the railroad terminal. These days the only rail passenger service was provided by AMTRAK. The famous "City of New Orleans" made a southbound stop every morning and a northbound stop in the late afternoon. I made a mental note to make a date with Laura for a train trip to New Orleans and the French Quarter one weekend soon. We passed under the railroad viaduct and cruised by the Iron Horse Grill, the old Armour Meat House that had been converted into a popular restaurant. My favorite item on that menu was the shrimp enchiladas.

As we crossed Gallatin Street, Dallas said that tonight we were just going to cruise around and see what we could see. I told him that sounded good to me. Pearl Street became West Pearl Street as we crossed Pascagoula, and the character of the area changed from one hundred percent commercial to a mixture of mostly residential and only some commercial. It appeared that there were more boarded-up houses than not. We passed by the Summers Hotel on our left. The front door of The Subway Lounge was open.

Dallas eased the Lexus onto an unnamed street on the right. As we approached the first intersection, he said softly, "Well, I'll be damned."

His eyes were squinting, as he leaned forward almost over the steering wheel.

"What is it?" I asked.

"Three weeks ago there would be at least six dealers on this corner competing for our business," he replied.

It looked deserted tonight. As we pulled up to the stop sign, a dull silver van crossed in front of us. It too had dark tinted windows, so it was impossible to see the driver. It had the appearance of a delivery van, more than a passenger van, with no windows on the side or rear. Dallas waited a half-minute for the van to travel half a block up the street and said, "Let's observe this guy awhile." He turned off the headlights of the Lexus and made a slow left turn. There was no other traffic in sight. We were now three-quarters of a short city block behind the van. It appeared that it was traveling very slowly, as if searching for an address. Most of the street lights had been shot out, causing it to be rather dark. The silver van stopped at the next intersection—maybe sixty yards in front of us. Dallas shifted the Lexus automatic transmission to neutral and let the car coast. His right arm raised up, and then went down between the bucket seats to the back seat, where he grabbed a pair of binoculars. He handed them to me, and told me to get a number. I raised the glasses to my eyes, quickly adjusted them and reported, "Alabama OM1 4J7." As the van made a right turn, the numbers went out of focus. Dallas picked up his police walkie talkie and requested that a patrol car respond to our area to make a traffic stop on the van.

"Four Bravo Four. I'm only two blocks away. What's his twenty?"

"Four Bravo Four, this is Unit Two. He's turning right onto Robinson Road. Silver van. Alabama plates."

We also turned right onto Robinson Road, continuing to maintain our half-block cushion behind the van. Robinson Road is a four-lane undivided main traffic artery. Usually busy during the day, traffic was light at the moment. In a minute and a half, a white JPD cruiser with blue lights on its roof and a blue and gold stripe down its side passed us on the left and then eased in behind the van. The cruiser followed its target closely for two blocks, both maintaining a speed of thirty-five miles per hour, five miles per hour slower than the posted limit.

When the blue lights of Four Bravo Four came on and began rotating, the van merely maintained its pace, as if the police car was not really twenty feet behind it. There was a sharp yelp of the cruiser's electronic siren—only one blast. Still no response from the van. We were now three car lengths behind Four Bravo Four and approaching West Capitol Street, another four-lane traffic artery that fed into downtown. As the van completed a right turn onto West Capitol, its back doors swung open. Standing in the doorway of the van was a man dressed in what appeared to be green military combat fatigues and a Marine-style baseball cap with a gold circle on its front. In his hands was an automatic weapon that resembled an AK-47, the Russian assault rifle. Holding the weapon at his hip, he opened rounds of automatic fire into the windshield of the police car, the orange flash bursts lighting up his face. All I could tell was that he was a white male between twenty-five and forty-five with crew cut hair. Glass exploded from the front of the police car as it swerved violently to the left. It straightened for an instant, then crashed almost headlong into a utility pole. Upon impact, the car, with smoke coming from its skidding tires, spun counterclockwise and slammed sideways into the brick and glass front of a barber shop. I could see Four Bravo Four's limp head bang backward into the headrest, even though an airbag had deployed upon impact with the telephone pole.

In such cases, human instinct takes over. We could have probably continued the chase, and ultimately somehow stopped the van. But we needed to be on the scene of the accident, administering first aid, calling for an ambulance and whatever else was necessary. Dallas radioed for immediate assistance, gave a description of the van, and then pulled over to the marked police cruiser. As we got out of the Lexus and saw the uniformed officer behind the wheel, we knew it was too late. In moments, the ambulance arrived and the scene turned into a carnival of blue lights and squelching radio talk among police who needed something to do to avenge the death of a fellow officer. Roadblocks went up all over Jackson in an attempt to catch the van and its occupants. It was to no avail.

Chapter 16

Up until now, it had been a game. No, not a game. A play. A drama. Like something one would see at New Stage Theater. My part in the play was the gullible investigator, intrigued and fascinated with meeting prominent Jacksonians such as Walter Fox and Timothy Tyler, mayoral candidates, Alvin Porter, JBA President, and Dennis Davis, television news personality. I was used by others to suit their purposes.

I had been taken in by it all. Yesterday, I felt as giddy as a sophomore who had been asked out by an upper-class cheerleader. I was circulating among the high and mighty of Jackson. I was somebody. It wasn't like that when I was simply an average high school student in the Jackson Public Schools, not so many years ago. I had been seduced by it all.

Now it was the morning after, when reality takes the place of the dreams of the night before. But in this case, the dreams were real, and the images were burned in my mind like a hot brand on a Texas steer. I summoned all my mental tricks, but still could not escape the scene that kept replaying in my mind—the burst of gunfire from the AK-47, the exploding windshield, the screeching tires, and the limp head of Four Bravo Four.

This mental torture had happened to me before. My

first brush with it came during my rookie year on the force in St. Louis. While on uniformed patrol during a midnight shift, I had received a call to check out a report of kids popping firecrackers. When I arrived at the location, the parking lot of an office building, I encountered a car occupied by a hysterical woman who told me that her boyfriend had killed himself. After I got her somewhat calmed down, she told me that he had been depressed all day, and while they were riding around in her car, he had put a gun in his mouth and threatened to blow his brains out right in front of her. Apparently, he had been mixed up in a burglary ring and was about to be arrested. She said that he went behind the building, and then she had heard a shot. I told her to wait in the car while I checked out the back of the building. It was a cold winter night, and I was not prepared for what I was to find. There, laying face down, was the body of a man. Between his legs was a gun, a service revolver just like the kind holstered on my hip. But what I was to see in my sleep for the next two weeks was the top of his head that had been blown apart, and the gray, blue and red matter mixed with hair from which steam rose into the crisp, cold air of the night.

It turned out that the man was a police officer from another town, and had been involved with a burglary ring. He was the desk sergeant and took calls from residents who notified the police when they were going to be out of town. He then passed along the addresses of the vacant houses to others in the ring, who would burglarize the place while the owner was gone. The ring had been busted, somebody had talked, and tomorrow was the day of reckoning. It took a long time for the incident to recede from my memory.

Today, after having spent twenty years of my life as a sworn upholder of the law, it dawned on me that police officers call themselves by their unit numbers more than they do by their given names. Perhaps it is a type of self-defense mechanism. Some way to shield them from the pain and grief of a fellow officer's death while on the job. If such is the case, I can tell you that it doesn't work. Except for the immediate family, no one hurts more than other police officers when a brother or sister is killed in the line of duty. Fellow officers take it personally.

Psychologists have identified several stages of grief that people experience after the death of a loved one. Sometimes, in rare cases, it takes only a few days to go through the process. In others, it might take years. All I know is that I spent last night lying in bed, trying to exorcise images of death from my mind. Good sleep would not come. Just as soon as I would fall asleep, the scene from West Capitol Street would replay itself. Movies and television shows have a way of making such a scene appear entertaining. It adds to the plot. But there's one thing the Hollywood types cannot replicate on a screen—the smell of death. It is a vague, metallic scent, hard to describe, but unforgettable once it has been inhaled. In this case it included an odd mixture of gunfire smoke, burning rubber, antifreeze and the blood of a dying man puddling underneath him.

Today there would be newspaper and television stories about the events of last night. There would be a profile of the slain officer. I did not care for any of it. I wanted only one thing—to find the killer.

So, where would I begin? The leads were rather slim. There was a gray van, an Alabama tag, and a man with an AK-47. I thought about him for a moment. He was in his early fifties. What was unique about him? I visualized the scene again and focused on the details. I recalled no scars or marks. No unusual or distinguishing physical characteristics. Then it hit me. The cap. There was something unusual about the cap. Yes. There was a gold circle of some kind on the front of the cap. An identifying emblem, perhaps.

My thoughts were interrupted by the sound of the telephone. I was in no mood to talk to anybody yet. It was only 9:00 a.m. I figured that I might be in the talking mood by 5:00 p.m., but I couldn't guarantee that. I looked at the caller identification system on the top of my telephone and noticed that it was a call from Deputy Chief Dallas. I would take this call.

"Good morning, Jack," said Dallas, after I answered with a tired hello. "I have some information about last night that might be of interest to you."

"Go ahead," I said, perking up.

"The van was stolen two days ago in downtown Mobile, Alabama. It belongs to a laundry. There has been no trace of it since we saw it last night. Naturally, we have an APB out on it." He paused and let that information sink in before continuing. "This morning, we received another missing person report. The person who called was Mrs. Ruby Elmore, mother of a seventeen-year-old male named Willie Elmore. It seems that he did not come home last night. We sent a detective to personally interview her awhile ago, and he came up with some very interesting information. Willie's big buddy is one Garfield Gates. Both of them have been arrested on numerous occasions. Gates is even out on parole. When we checked at Gates' house, we learned that he didn't come home last night either. That's not unusual. While at the house, however, Garfield's younger brother came forward and told the detective that he saw Derrick and Rodney get into the back of a silver van as it drove away. He swears that they were pulled into the back of the van. The brother was watching from inside a vacant house on the corner, probably managing their supply of crack. All three of them are known street dealers."

"It makes sense," I said.

"It also explains why those toads in the van would risk killing a police officer who was attempting to pull them over."

"That's right," I replied with enlightenment. "The auto theft is minor, compared to kidnapping. That brings up one other thing."

"What's that?"

"Interstate transportation of a stolen motor vehicle and kidnapping are federal offenses," I pointed out. "The FBI would then have jurisdiction."

"They are on the way over here right now," he said.

"That's good," I replied. "That should take some pressure off you guys with the media. By the way, did Four Bravo Four have a family?"

"Yes. He was one of five children. He has four sisters. He was the only son. He also has a pregnant wife and a two year old baby girl. They are all taking it hard, as you would imagine. He was a damn good police officer."

"Can I do anything?" I asked.

"His children will need an education."

I said good-bye and hung up the receiver, even more melancholy than before. At the same time I was excited about the possibility of a reasonably good lead. Somebody in a stolen van, with Alabama license plates and a military or paramilitary connection, was probably kidnapping Jackson's street corner drug dealers. Within a minute, there was another telephone call. This time is was Laura.

"Did you hear what happened last night?" she asked.

"I not only heard about it. I was there," I said. I gave

her the highlights, and then told her about my conversation with Chief Dallas.

"Now you've got something to work with," she said somewhat triumphantly.

"How am I going to work with that?"

"You'll think of something," she said. "You're too smart. You'll leave no stone unturned."

"For what?"

"I don't know. Leads of some kind. Who knows? It might even be mercenaries or one of those paramilitary groups." She sounded enthusiastic. Like there had been some breakthrough. "Listen, I've got to go to a meeting. How about a night out to clear your mind? It is Friday, you know."

"I'll pick you up at six-thirty at your place. And dress casual. I'm in the mood for a Jackson Generals game."

I trudged to my back office and fired up my computer to check my e-mail, just in case there was some important message. There was none. I clicked around and checked today's news through an on-line news service that I subscribe to. Nothing much new there. Same old stuff going on the world. One news story caught my eye. It was about a paramilitary group that was making plans to secede from the United States. I decided to read more about this phenomenon of paramilitary right-wing organizations.

Chapter 17

It was exactly the kind of evening that I needed. Laura and I cruised to Smith-Wills Stadium in the Camaro and arrived at the playing of the national anthem. I bought two box seats behind home plate. On the way to our seats, we stopped at the concession stand for hot dogs, peanuts and cold beer. Later, I would have a chocolate and vanilla swirl frozen yogurt, served up in a miniature Los Angeles Dodgers plastic helmet.

Tonight the Generals were playing the Arkansas Travelers, the AA affiliate of the St. Louis Cardinals. The "Gens," as we locals called them, were affiliated with the Houston Astros. The next stop for a player on his way up to the majors was a stop at the AAA franchise in New Orleans, then on to the Astros. It was not uncommon for a player to go directly to the big club, but it did not happen often. The Generals had a right fielder who was leading the league in just about every category, and many in the know predicted that he would be playing with the Houston Astros before the year was over.

Although the current franchise was affiliated with the Houston Astros, Jackson actually became a Texas League town in 1975, when the New York Mets moved its AA team to the capital city. The team was known as the Jackson Mets. Unfortunately, I was not here then to see the likes of Daryl Strawberry, Lenny Dykstra,

Mookie Wilson and Wally Backman play their AA ball here. But I couldn't complain. I was in St. Louis, where the Cardinals played. I'm a fair baseball fan, getting out to see at least a dozen games each year. I confess to enjoying AA baseball more than major league baseball. I think it's because the players are trying so hard to make it. They also have not yet been corrupted by endorsements and such things as shoe contracts. After Jackson Generals games, the players still sign autographs and meet the kids. They still seem to play for the name on the front of the jersey, instead of the name on the back.

The game was a good one. Arkansas jumped to a 2-0 lead in the first, but Jackson tied it up in the fifth inning. Both teams went on hitting sprees, and by the end of the ninth inning it was tied 8-8. We yelled when our team got a hit, and screamed at the umpire on a close call at home. In the tenth inning, Laura brought me back to reality.

"So what's your next move?" she asked.

"I'm going to Mobile tomorrow," I said without hesitation.

"What?"

"Remember what you mentioned this morning? About using the Internet?"

"Yes," she said, now oblivious to the action on the field.

"I did some searching. I asked several different search engines to look for mercenaries, and I got back over eight hundred hits. When I looked into a bunch of sites, I realized they were all about the same mercenary video game. So I modified my search and asked for soldiers for hire. I got two hits." She was leaning forward in her chair. "One was in New York, and one was in— you guessed it—Mobile, Alabama."

"You mean you can hire mercenaries on the Internet! That's illegal," she replied with a voice that rose in volume with every word. An older couple in front turned around to see what the commotion was all about.

"Whoa. I'm not sure just yet. But they did require a credit card number, and a $50 fee to see the details of what they offer. After what I read on the computer screen, I'm convinced they will supply soldiers for any little mission one might have a need for."

"This is bizarre," said Laura.

"I agree. But I've got to check it out. I'm meeting one of their representatives in Mobile tomorrow afternoon."

"Let's go talk about this," she said, beginning to rise from her seat.

I put my arm on hers and said, "Wait just a few more minutes. The Generals have the bases loaded, and it's now the bottom of the tenth."

She sat back but did not watch the game, instead choosing to stare downward. There was a sharp crack of the bat and the crowd instantly roared. She flinched. I looked up to see the ball heading over left center field just to the right of the "Gas Gives You More For Your Money" sign. It was a grand slam home run. The Generals won 12 - 8. I felt it was a good omen.

We drove back to Laura's house and discussed the situation. I revealed to her that I had set up a meeting in a Mobile restaurant with someone who might have "some security forces" available on short notice. I assured her that I would be extremely cautious. We agreed that whomever I would meet would be either a real amateur or a real pro. I told her that I would keep in touch by cellular phone. She said she was not going to leave her house until I returned. Frankly, I did not see this trip as a very risky proposition. Laura felt otherwise. It showed in her goosebumps.

Chapter 18

Saturday morning at 8:00 a.m., I drove to a car rental agency on South State Street and rented a Ford Taurus with less than four thousand miles on the odometer. The Camaro remained behind in the parking lot of the agency. Even though it's in first-class mechanical shape, it is a rare event for me to drive that little, turquoise beauty outside the Jackson metropolitan area. There is no sense in getting too far from home in it, lest there be a breakdown that requires expert attention.

Mobile is about a three-hour drive from Jackson. That would put me there just before lunch and give me a little over an hour to kill before my 2:00 p.m. appointment with someone whose name I did not even know. Last night, Laura and I had decided that the person would either be an amateur or a pro. There was one other possibility, and that was that it was an Internet scam, and no one would show.

I headed south on Highway 49, a four-lane, unlimited access piece of Americana. It is one of Mississippi's most colorful but dangerous highways. The average driving speed is about sixty-five miles per hour, but there are no entrance/exit ramps, only intersections and driveways. The first town is Richland, a commercial, light industrial strip where eighteen-wheel tractor trailers get weighed and pull out in front of oncoming traffic. It is not as if they have a choice. That's just the only way they can get onto the road. Less than five miles further south is Florence, where stopping at the traffic signal is almost always a certainty. In between these two towns one can see colorful quilts for sale, palm reader signs, and a plethora of small businesses that certainly must be operated on the proverbial shoestring.

South of Florence, the road opens up to a more rural setting. A few miles later I drove by Piney Woods Country Life School, and a cover-alled man parked in a side road selling syrup from a van. D'Lo, Mendenhall, Magee, and Mt. Olive were put behind me in short order. I almost did a double-take when I passed a road sign that proclaimed "Dry Creek Water Park" just ahead to the right. I made a mental note to take a photo of that sign and send it to Jay Leno for his Monday night "Headlines" show.

There is no shortage of roadside stands in this part of Highway 49. Most of them sell fruits and vegetables, a few adding antiques and junk. Mostly junk. This time of year, the watermelons are coming in, and they are plentiful and cheap along this stretch of highway. The best melons in the world are grown in Sullivan's Hollow, a community not too far east of the highway. I decided I would stop and get one on my return trip. Among the southern foods I enjoy eating most in summer are watermelon, boiled peanuts, and boiled shrimp. All can be found on the side of Highway 49 in south Mississippi. Add to those another one of my favorite summertime delicacies—the tomato sandwich.

Tomato sandwiches are best when vine-ripened tomatoes are sliced and placed between two mayonnaise-laced pieces of what's called "light bread" in the South. Salt and pepper are added to taste, and it is delicious with an ice-cold glass of milk. People in St. Louis would say "yuck" to such a sandwich, but I was raised on them and still eat them often. All it takes for a southerner to appreciate the South is to move away from the food. Sickness sets in quickly. Homesickness.

I paused in Hattiesburg for a soft drink, then continued on down Highway 49 to Highway 98, which went directly to Mobile. Arriving at Mobile at noon, I drove around for a while, then gassed up the rental car. I scouted out our designated meeting place, a restaurant near Interstate 10 and Mobile Bay. The small number of cars in the parking lot told me that the lunch crowd had probably thinned out.

I walked in, told the hostess that there would be two of us, and was ushered to a blue, vinyl-covered booth along the back wall. The wall to my right was solid plate glass from floor to ceiling, offering a view of the USS Alabama Memorial Park and Mobile Bay just beyond. In the park were a variety of aircraft on permanent display. The tail of a B-52 Flying Fortress dominated the view of the park. Near it was what appeared to be an SR-71 Blackbird, the fastest plane in the world. On just about every available wall space in the restaurant was a framed photograph or drawing of a military aircraft. If I didn't know better, I'd have thought that I was at the Officers Club at some naval base.

I felt a hand press just a little too hard on my left shoulder. I looked up to see a rugged looking man of about fifty-five wearing khaki pants and a khaki shirt. He had a crew cut, and was deeply tanned, the look of someone who was around water and sun a lot. He had on a sly smile—make that a grin—as he plopped down in the booth.

"So you're interested in recruiting some men for a job, are you?"

The accent sounded Californian. He leaned forward. I looked him in the eye and said, "That's correct."

"What kind of a job?"

"A lot of security guard work mostly," I was making this up as I went along. I hoped that in a moment I'd be the one asking the questions.

"More details," he said.

"My client is shipping some goods about ninety miles into Mexico by truck. I want to make certain that the merchandise gets there. The conventional security guard companies don't seem to be interested. Can't say as I blame them. The banditos are getting good at truck hijackings. I'll need some good security that knows how to handle possible action involving weapons." I hoped this sounded convincing. I reminded myself that I was the customer, and that he wanted my business. "Is that something your company can handle?"

"Not a problem," he replied. "How many men you need and when you need 'em?"

I told him that I'd need at least twenty and that we planned to make the trip in about three weeks. I also told him that there may be other trips. He told me that the fee would be $500 per day, per man. I told him that would be no problem.

"What other kinds of jobs do your men do?" I asked.

"You name it and we do it. No job too large or small, as they say."

I asked what the biggest job was that he had ever done, and he told me right away that was confidential. I then asked if obeying the law was in his company's training manual.

"Like I said, we get the job done, no matter what. What's illegal in one country may be legal in another."

"What's your name?" I asked.

"Vernon," he replied

No matter how hard I pried I couldn't get any more information about him or his company. I told him that I would get back to him in a day or two. He gave me a card on which was printed "Mercenaries For Hire—No job too small or large." There was a Mobile post office box number and a telephone number.

He got up and walked out the front door. No good-bye, see ya' later or nothing. It was if he could take my business, or leave it. Still, I had the feeling that he meant what he said. Nothing seemed beyond this burly mercenary broker, if indeed that's what he was. I left two dollars on the table and went to the plate glass front door that faced the parking lot. I watched him get into a Hum-Vee of all things, that modern military version of a jeep that gets its nickname from its abbreviation—HMMWV. Those initials stand for High Mobility Multipurpose Wheeled Vehicle. Such vehicles were now sold commercially. His was painted dull green, just enough that one could tell it was the civilian version. As he backed out of his parking place, he put a cap on his head. I recognized it immediately—I had seen it before. It was a marine baseball cap with a gold circle on the front. The same type of cap that I had seen on the killer of Four Bravo Four back in Jackson. I let him get almost out of the parking lot, then scampered to my rental car. I had to follow this guy. There weren't many caps like that one.

He negotiated the traffic and pulled out onto Interstate 10, heading west to the Bankhead Tunnel. I stayed about six car lengths behind, and put two cars between us. We went through the tunnel, continued west on I-10, then north on I-65 . He exited at Highway 98 and motored on toward Mississippi. The road was four lane all the way, and it was fairly easy to trail him.

He maintained the speed limit, and seemed oblivious to the fact that I was following him. We crossed the Escatawpa River and encountered a "WELCOME TO MISSISSIPPI" sign. Tagged onto its bottom was a smaller, blue sign that read, "Only Positive Mississippi Spoken Here." About one-fourth of a mile past the Escatawpa, the Hum-Vee made a left onto a one-lane, gravel and sand road to the left. I kept going, keeping my head straight, but cutting my eyes in that direction to take in all I could see. I couldn't see much, except the woods were thick, and the road was narrow.

I drove on for about a quarter-mile, then turned around and came back to the road. My sixth sense told me it was not a good idea to drive down that road. That left the next best thing. I drove down toward the river and pulled into a small roadside park—one of those that has only a picnic table and a litter barrel. I got out and walked back to the dirt road. The road was worn in such a way to indicate that it had gotten a fair amount of traffic lately. My head told me it was best to turn around, go back to Jackson, and tell the feds about this. My instincts told me time was of the essence.

Chapter 19

I began walking down the tree-canopied lane, with its thick woods on either side. Hanging moss draped the branches of the larger live-oaks. Although the scene would normally be picturesque, two things took away from its beauty—the increasingly incessant whine of mosquitoes around my ears, and the sound of gunfire coming from deep in the woods.

I recognized the gunfire sounds immediately, from the pattern of the shooting. It was a rifle range. No mistake about it. My thoughts went back to my Army Basic Training days at Fort Benning, Georgia, when the range leader would yell out: "Ready on the right? Ready on the left? Ready on the firing line? Commence firing." Three minutes later, after scores of volleys, the cry would ring out, "Cease firing." Then a few minutes to reload, and do it all over again. This was the firing pattern I now detected.

I walked a little slower, and a little closer to the right side of the road. Up ahead, the road curved sharply to the left. As I made the curve, I immediately encountered a silver, four-inch metal bar across the road. Hanging from its center was a sign that proclaimed, "No trespassing. Violators will be shot. Survivors will be prosecuted." I got the feeling that this sign was not just for show. Nevertheless, I stepped over the bar and continued down the road. The firing range noise was now to my right and becoming louder. It couldn't be more than fifty yards away. I reached up and felt the back of my neck. The welts from the mosquito bites were getting larger. The road made another bend, this time to the right.

I walked into the compound before I realized it. There were three wooden buildings about sixteen feet by twenty feet in size, and two others that were half that. Their appearance was old and weathered. In the middle was a cleared area, where a twenty-foot, metal flagpole held high a limp United States flag. The ground was a mixture of sand and dirt. My guess was that it was a camp of some kind. The river would be just beyond the buildings. Two Hummers were parked by one of the smaller buildings. Fortunately for me, the camp was deserted. No, not deserted. That is when someone leaves, never intending to come back. This camp was vacant.

I stood still and listened. Over the din of the mosquitoes, I heard a whimpering sound in one of the buildings. As the sound grew louder, I realized that it was someone crying. I moved over to the building and peered through the screened window. There, sitting on the bare floor, was a boy-man. I'd guess him to be eighteen years old. He was black and had close-cropped hair. He was wearing only military fatigue pants. No shirt or shoes. He was handcuffed to one of the dozen metal-frame bunk beds lined up in two rows, barrack-style. He saw my shadow on the floor at the same time

I did. He stopped sobbing, looked at the window where I was standing, and gasped. It took him a second to process whether I was friend or foe.

"Help me, mister. Please help me," he whispered loudly in desperation.

I walked around to the front of the building and stepped inside. He was frantic.

"They're sending us to Africa! Tonight! Got to get away! Please help!"

I put my fingers to my lips and said, "Shhh. Go slow and tell me."

"They kidnapped us. They've been making us learn to be soldiers. They're sending us to Africa—to die! Please help me, mister!"

Suddenly his eyes changed. The look on his face went from frantic to panic. I could read those eyes as easy as I could a John Grisham novel. And what they said was—someone is behind you. I turned around and saw Vernon, the man from the café, standing in the doorway. He was now dressed in camouflage, military fatigues, complete with jungle combat boots, and the cap with the gold circle on the front. His outfit also included an AK-47, which he held at port arms across his chest.

"Well, I see you want to learn a little more about our organization," he said sarcastically.

"You might say that," I replied.

"And just what would you like to know?"

"Is what he said the truth?" I asked, pointing at the young man on the floor.

"What we have here is an all-volunteer army," he said, looking at me hard between the eyes. "They have chosen to go on a mission of great importance to their country of duty. They will be paid very well for their services."

"What about this one?" I asked. "He doesn't seem like much of a volunteer."

"Yes. Such a pity."

"And what might their so-called country of duty be?" I asked, adding as much sarcasm as I could muster, under the circumstances.

"That's none of your business." He turned his head and yelled out, "Sergeant!"

I heard the running footsteps across the yard that grew louder until the door burst open and a man in his late twenties, dressed in the same manner as Vernon, charged in. His haircut was also close cut in the military style found in boot camp. He carried no weapon in his hands, but I noticed a Marine bayonet holstered on his belt.

"Yes sir."

"Secure this intruder to the bunk," barked Vernon. "Stay with him until further notice. I'm going down to the firing range to see that the day's training exercises are finished. We'll be moving out at midnight. If he gives you any trouble, handle him as you would any other criminal who is caught breaking and entering."

Vernon walked out the door, leaving the so-called sergeant to carry out his orders. With a vise-like grip he grabbed my wrist and handcuffed it to the closest bed frame. He turned around, stepped to a corner of the cabin, did an about-face and sat down on the floor in a yoga-like position.

Chapter 20

Three hours later, we were still there. The sergeant was in his corner, I was cuffed to one bed, and the kid was cuffed to another. The kid still looked like he was in a state of shock. The shadows had grown longer, and darkness was descending on the camp. Vernon returned to the other cabin, but left us with Vernon, Jr. The only time our guard had moved was to reach up and pull a string to turn on a naked light bulb overhead.

What were they going to do with me? I tried to put myself in Vernon's place. His alternatives were to leave me handcuffed to the bunk, handcuff me to something more permanent, take me with him, or simply kill me.

I evaluated the choices. Leaving me handcuffed to the bunk would mean my freeing myself within fifteen minutes. Even though I might not be able to get out of the cuffs, it would be easy to gain mobility. At worst, I would have to carry the end of the bunk bed with me. This alternative ranked low. Handcuffing me to something more permanent, such as a tree, made more sense. It would probably be at least morning, maybe a day or two, before anyone would find me. That would be plenty of time to get far away from here. Even if I called out the Cavalry, where would I call it out to? There was, of course, the alternative of killing the prisoner. Disposal of the body would not be an issue, since everyone would be leaving the area. This might not be preferable, but it was available. Then it dawned on me. Vernon had killed a police officer. Killing me would be a minor inconvenience to someone like him.

So, those were the choices. Which one would he make? Killing me and handcuffing me to the tree were the logical choices. I decided to give myself some leeway. One thing most police officers, whether active or retired, carry on their keychain is a handcuff key. I couldn't reach in my pocket, however, because Vernon, Jr. was standing watch over us, more like a statue than a guard dog. I needed a diversion. There was the ole "having a heart attack" trick, but this guy would just let me die. I considered spitting in the kid's face in an attempt to make him angry, but all that would do is provide entertainment for one guard. Maybe there was something else that would faze him.

"Hey, kid," I said, turning to my fellow prisoner. "What country are they going to send you to?"

His eyes were wide, even though he was much calmer. It was doubtful he could answer any question about the operation. I tried another tack.

"I saw your mother the other day," I said in a matter-of-fact tone.

That got his attention. "Where?" he demanded.

"On the steps of City Hall. There was a press conference about you and your missing friends. The FBI has been brought into the case."

Vernon, Jr. remained stone-faced. The pigeons

would have loved him. The kid, however, was now coming back to his senses. He got up on one knee.

"Is the FBI coming?" he asked.

"No," I replied. "They are going to wait until the group is away from here before making their move. My guess is that it will be at the airport."

When I said the word "airport," Vernon, Jr. did an about face and walked purposefully out the screen door. He ran across the yard to a small, wooden building where Vernon was, no doubt, making serious departure plans. It was time to use the handcuff key. With my left hand, I dug into my pants pocket and retrieved my key ring. I quickly inserted the key into the handcuff that was around my wrist and twisted. The cuff instantly came undone. The kid watched excitedly, and began bobbing up and down in a crouched position.

The screen door on the other house made a loud creaking noise as it opened. I jumped up and hit the light bulb with my open hand. It popped loudly. The cabin went dark, but was penetrated by the light from the center of the yard. We could see the shadow of Vernon and Junior in their military fatigues, walking briskly toward our cabin. Both had guns. The kid started whimpering again, and I told him to "shut up and tell them that I went out the door," hoping that he could talk to them.

I rolled across the floor, then jumped up and grabbed an open rafter. I pulled myself up, and lay on it like lying on a small log across a gorge far above a river. The would-be soldiers came in and stood in front of the kid, whose face was reflected in the ray of light coming in from outside. There was a gleam from the open handcuff on the frame of the bunk bed. They just stood there, very still, for a few seconds, heads turning around, bodies still. I prayed that they would not look up. Strangely, a drop of what I perceived to be perspiration collected at the bottom of my hand and fell to the floor, less than six inches behind the combat boots of Vernon.

Vernon leaned his head down to within six inches of the kid's face and screamed, "Where is he?"

The kid slinked back as if about to be hit, and said in a whiny voice, "He went out the door." As he spoke the words, he nodded toward the door behind the two men.

"Go get the other sergeants," barked Vernon to the younger man, who turned and headed out the door. He ran to the other cabin and scrambled inside. Vernon was standing still, listening, like a deer hunter in a tree stand who has heard movement in the woods. My chest was about to burst. My breathing was slow, so as to be silent, but I needed oxygen desperately. Another drop of liquid fell from my hand to the wood floor.

This time Vernon heard the splat, turned around and looked down. I rolled off the rafter and fell on top of Vernon, knocking him to the floor. I managed to get one arm around his neck, and hold onto him from behind.

We were scuffling on the floor, four feet in front of the bed frame. He tried shaking me off by making quick jerks to the left, then to the right. I attempted to pull us over toward the kid, in the hope that he might help. Suddenly, the bright flash of bullets exploding from the muzzle of Vernon's AK-47 lit up the cabin. The noise was deafening. I put more pressure on my hold around his neck, got my legs around his waist and squeezed with all my strength. I was a cowboy riding a wild bronco, holding on for dear life. Another short burst of automatic fire from the rifle, as our bodies rolled over and over, smashing into the bed frame. The bullets tore into the side of the cabin, making holes in the siding and in the screens. There was an abrupt scream from the kid, and I saw him stand up over us, lifting the metal bed frame over his head. He slammed the leg of the metal frame down squarely on Vernon's right ear. An animal-like grunt erupted from the man at the impact. I felt him go limp and heard the gun fall to the floor.

I extracted myself and grabbed for the gun. I clasped the barrel with one hand, and pulled it toward me. There was resistance. The kid had the butt of the gun. Vernon lay unconscious beneath us. Our eyes met. It seemed for a second to be a stand-off. The kid had one end of the weapon, I had the other. But he was still handcuffed to the bed frame. Across the way, the screen door from the other building made the familiar squeaking noise. I glanced in that direction. As I did so, the kid jerked the gun, and it slipped from my right hand as if there were some kind of oil on the barrel. Instinctively, I looked down at my right hand, and immediately saw why I had lost my grip. My hand was covered with blood. It must have been cut when I smashed the light bulb. What had dripped down behind Vernon's boots a few moments ago was not perspiration, it was blood.

The kid now held the AK-47 with his right hand on the trigger and the barrel in his left hand. It was an awkward position. I knew the kid had no reason to kill me, and probably would not do so. I also knew that he was not about to give up the gun.

"Fire over toward that building," I whispered loudly. "He's coming out the door."

The kid looked in that direction, and without hesitation or aim, fired a short burst in the direction of the other cabin. The bullets tore through the screen of our cabin and slammed into the outside wall of the other building. The screen door closed on the other building. Vernon, Jr. had retreated back inside.

"I'm going for help," I told the kid. "Keep him pinned down in that cabin."

"No," said the kid forcefully, turning the automatic rifle on me.

I had forgotten how large the hole was at the end of a rifle barrel when one is looking at it from the receiving end. Even in the semi-darkness, it looked larger than I knew it really was.

"There's a phone in that building where that other man is," he said, gesturing with his hand. "Call those FBI men, and tell them to get here right now from that airport in Mobile."

I did not think it was a good idea to inform him that I had made up the part about the FBI and the airport. Help was a long way away, but I was in no condition to discuss the point. I reached into my pocket and pulled out my key ring. He moved the gun aside as I reached up to unlock his handcuff. He was now free from the bed frame, with an AK-47 in his hands. I guessed he would be out the door and down the road.

He looked at me and said, "Okay, here's what we're going to do. You're going to go around to the back of that house, and I'm gonna get him to come out. When he does, you go inside and call for help."

It sounded like a decent plan to me. Crawling over the still unconscious Vernon, I duck-walked over to the cabin door, and opened it. It squeaked loudly, and was suddenly on the receiving end of a burst of gunfire from the other cabin. No rounds found their way to me. From behind me came the deafening burst of return gunfire from the kid.

"Get going!" he commanded in a loud whisper.

I crashed out the door and ran for a large live-oak tree ten yards ahead. It looked to be six feet in diameter, certainly large enough to protect me from the bullets. More gunfire, as the dirt behind me splattered up. As I reached the safety of the tree, I heard and felt bullets penetrating the skin of the oak on the opposite side. Still more automatic gunfire. This time, a burst from the kid. I remained behind the tree for what seemed like three minutes, the mosquitoes humming like dive bombers past my ears, feasting on my exposed flesh.

From the third cabin on the other side of the yard, I heard the kid's voice yell, "Come get me, honky!" It was answered with gunfire in his direction. That was my cue to circle around to the back of the cabin occupied by Junior. The kid was now yelling and ducking, while Junior was taking pot shots where he thought his target might be. I reached the back of the building and saw that Junior was occupied with the kid. There was a front door and a back door. Junior was standing inside the front door, while I was standing outside the back door. I scanned the large room.

Then I saw it. The orange light of a battery recharger, holding in its cradle the most lovely cellular telephone I have ever seen. It was only two feet inside the door. It would be an easy grab to snatch it. However, if Junior turned around while I was snatching the phone, I would be less than fifteen feet from him. My only chance was to grab it while he was busy shooting at the kid.

It did not take long for the shootout to intensify. I waited until the split second when Junior fired a burst, then gently opened the screen door, and lifted the cellular phone from its source of energy. The odor of gunpowder was strong, as the spent shells bounced on the wooden floor. Unexpectedly, he stopped shooting. I froze. Please kid, fire back. My plea was answered instantly, as bullets tore into the ceiling. It dawned on me that the kid was intentionally shooting high.

As Junior responded with another burst, I eased the door shut, and retreated to the safety of my previous position behind the live-oak tree. I sat down with my back leaning on the tree, and my legs straight out on the ground. I flipped open the cell phone and dialed Laura's number, knowing she would be anxiously sitting by her telephone. I pressed "send" and heard the ringing sound, then the click of an answer. It was the voice of Laura.

"Hello. You've reached the voice mailbox of Laura Webster. I'm away from the phone right now and can't take your call. At the tone, please leave me a message, and I'll call you when I return."

Then there was a beep. This was incredible! Here I was, in the middle of a gun battle in the deep woods of south Mississippi, and I get a recording. I talked as loudly as I could into the phone, but low enough that Junior could not hear me between bursts.

"Laura, call out the Cavalry, A-S-A-P! Escatawpa River at Highway 98! Paramilitary group that . . ."

I did not have a chance to finish the sentence.

Standing beside me was Vernon, his ear bloodied and the look of hate in his eyes. In his hand he held a .45 caliber pistol, and it was pointed at my head.

Chapter 21

"You have one more call to make," said Vernon in a stern voice.

He took the cell phone with his left hand, still holding the pistol to my head with the other hand. Using his thumb, he pressed the "RCL" button. Laura's number appeared on the face of the phone in a glow of green light.

"Say that you were kidding, and that you will talk to her later." He pressed the "SEND" button and placed the phone to my ear.

"Hello," said Laura.

"Disregard my previous call," I said slowly and deliberately. "I'll tell you about it when I get back to Capitol Arms."

Vernon then flipped the phone shut and placed it in his pocket. Just then, I heard the squeak of the screen door opening from the main cabin. The gunfire had stopped. Junior walked over to the tree.

"I finally got the bastard," he said to Vernon.

"Good," Vernon replied. "Now take this sack of scum to the river, and make sure that he takes an underwater swim and never comes up."

Junior reached down and produced a flashlight from his back pocket. He pointed the light into the woods, just across the road and said, "Follow that trail."

I got up and did as he said. The woods were not very

thick with undergrowth, and the ground was as much sand as it was dirt. The trail was four feet wide in most places, and was straight as an arrow. Junior stayed about six feet behind me and kept the light shining over my shoulder, ahead of me. My plan was to simply jump into the river and swim away underwater. It occurred to me, however, that there was only a fifty-fifty chance that the river would be over my head. I tried to recall what it looked like from the roadway earlier, but could not visualize it. That meant I had only one chance. And now was the time to take it.

I put on the world's best acting job of tripping on a root and falling down. I lay there and moaned, as Junior moved to a crouched position and aimed his gun and flashlight right between my eyes. I began getting up very slowly, while clutching my left ankle with my left hand. My right hand was on the ground, bracing me as I rose. When I got about halfway up, I threw a handful of dirt and sand toward where I thought Junior's face would be. As I did so, I lunged straight at him, aiming my head at his chest. My head hit its mark, and knocked the wind out of him as he fell backward, with me on top of him. We struggled for his AK-47, but he held onto it like a lap bar on a thrill ride. The barrel was now between our faces as we struggled on the ground.

I'm not exactly sure how it happened, but the assault rifle discharged. A single shot. I felt the powder burn on my face, and thought that the bullet had grazed my cheek. Junior went limp.

Slowly, I picked up the flashlight from the ground and shined it in Junior's face. Déjà vu came over me. The top of his head was gone, just like the suicide case I had seen years ago as a rookie police officer.

I grabbed the rifle and headed back toward the camp, leaving Junior's body where it lay in the trail. The truck with the so-called soldiers would be coming through the base camp soon. My guess was that there would be at least one of Vernon's men for each "volunteer." Even an AK-47 assault rifle would be no match for a heavily armed squad of trained killers. I had to come up with a diversion. My first thought was to simply hide behind a tree and shoot out the tires as the truck passed by. The only problem with that plan is that the flash from the gun would give away my position and I would be a dead man within seconds. It would have to be something else.

Up ahead, I could see the light of the camp about fifty yards away. I cut off the flashlight and walked cautiously along. The mosquitoes were worse than ever. As I reached the road, I saw Vernon's silhouette in the main building. He was talking on the cellular phone at a voice level that I had no trouble hearing.

"Load them up right now," he barked. "We are moving out this very minute. We can't wait until midnight, as planned. I'll be waiting at the base camp. Get a move on."

I looked at Vernon's Hummer parked beside the building, and got my big idea. It was risky, but if it worked, it would delay the group's departure. Vernon was now talking to someone else on the cell phone, pacing back and forth as he did so. He could not see me in the darkness, but I had a perfect view of him. I crept up beside the Hum-Vee and slowly opened the driver's door. I stuck my foot inside and pressed down on the clutch while pulling the gearshift into neutral. The ground was level, soft dirt, and there was manageable resistance as I pushed this souped-up sport utility vehicle into the middle of the road, effectively blocking the path of any other vehicle. I reached under the dash and jerked loose every wire that I could find. I walked slowly backward into the woods behind me, keeping my eyes on Vernon. When I was about one hundred feet from the Hummer, I bumped into a huge live-oak tree. I climbed up about twenty-five feet and positioned myself on a limb that ran out, opposite the side of the camp. Even if he shined a light directly at me from the camp I would not be seen. On the other hand, if a group of searchers fanned out looking for me, and shined a light up the tree from any other angle, I was a dead man.

My thoughts were interrupted by the sound and lights of an approaching vehicle coming from deep in the woods down the road. It was a large, orange moving van, and it pulled up to the Hum-Vee parked in its path. The horn sounded and the driver yelled, "Get out here, and let's go!"

Vernon came out from the building and surveyed the situation. I heard them talking, but could not quite make out what they were saying. Vernon pointed toward the trail, then climbed into the Hummer. He reached down, and turned the ignition. It would not start. He yelled toward the moving van, and three men in military fatigues jumped out and pushed the vehicle back to its original spot beside the building. The men jumped back into the rear of the truck, and Vernon pounced into the cab. The big van drove away toward the highway.

I could not think of anything else to do, so I just sat there, straddled on a limb of a moss-draped live-oak, drenched in perspiration, mosquitoes buzzing in my ears. I felt my heart pounding inside my chest, as if trying to escape from the body to which it had been working overtime, supplying oxygen for the past few hours. I felt like I had just gotten off one of those movie thrill rides in an Orlando, Florida, theme park and walked out to find myself all alone, the park shut down and deserted. It had all been so real, yet so illusory. But it was not over.

Five minutes later, I heard gunfire in the direction of Highway 98. It lasted only a minute or so, but it was intense. There was automatic weapons fire. Lots of it. Then there would be only single shots. I pictured several Mississippi State Troopers attempting to take on a small army. Finally, the shooting stopped. I remained on the limb and waited.

It seemed like half an hour before headlights appeared on the dirt road from Highway 98. First, there were two cars that drove into the camp. I could only make out that they were large cars, dark in color. A moment later, I saw a sight that thrilled my soul—blue lights flashing brilliantly atop a police car, coming through the woods toward the camp. I shimmied down the tree, walked through the woods to the camp and yelled out as I approached.

The commanding officer was a Mississippi Highway Safety Patrol Sergeant. I briefed him on what had happened, as I knew it. I told him about the kid. We went over to where the young warrior had been, and found his body. The kid was probably a drug dealer with a long criminal record, but he had saved my life. I would make sure his family knew that he died doing something honorable.

The rest of the evening was a blur. Most of it was spent at the Mobile FBI office. I learned that this was part of a much larger organization supplying mercenaries to several rebel groups in Africa. The modus operandi was the same in several cities—kidnap street drug dealers, put them to sleep with a drug, then brainwash them for a week in a military camp setting. They would actually choose to go to Africa, rather than return to their neighborhoods. That is, all but one. And he was dead. While I waited at the FBI office, they conducted a raid at the Mobile airport, where a large cargo plane was seized, and several arrests were made. Similar raids were conducted later that evening at airports in Tampa, Florida, Charlotte, North Carolina and Atlanta.

I was exhausted, and decided it was best to spend the night in Mobile. After checking into a local motel, I went to the room and picked up the telephone. There were three telephone calls to make. The first was to Laura. I kept the details to a minimum, and told her that whatever she did—whomever she called—sure saved the day. I promised to give her a blow-by-blow account tomorrow. The second call was to Deputy Chief Tom Dallas, to whom I talked much longer. The third was to Dennis Davis. I told him that he was wrong about Pete and Repeat doing the kidnapping, and then referred him to the Mobile FBI and the Mississippi Highway Safety Patrol. He would get a good scoop. I wanted to maintain good relations with him, knowing that our paths would cross in the future.

The next morning, I drove back to Jackson, and was at Laura's front door by 10:00 a.m. Even though I was sore from the previous night's events, I wanted to get out today. We opted for brunch at the Olde Tyme Delicatessen in northeast Jackson. I was craving their cheese blintzes. We lingered there almost two hours, as I gave her the promised detailed account of the previous evening.

We then spent two hours just riding around in the Camaro. We circumnavigated the Barnett Reservoir by way of the Natchez Trace to Highway 16, then to Highway 25, and back across Spillway Road. We stopped at Overlook Point on the Trace and for half an hour watched the sailboats skimming across the water with their sails full out. It was like watching strokes of paint being applied to a seascape canvas. Then we went back into town, and rode out Robinson Road to the site of the old Shoney's Restaurant in Westland Plaza. We recalled our high school days, when cars came from all over town to enter the congested parking lot parade for the purpose of simply seeing and being seen.

"Hey," Laura said enthusiastically. "Let's go to the zoo."

For the next two hours, that's exactly what we did. Jackson's zoo is one of the best in the South. The chimpanzee entertained us with his antics, peacocks strutted around us, and the magnificent giraffes put on a stretching show for us. We had hamburgers and soft drinks at the zoo café and acted like high school kids again. It was just the kind of day that I needed, to help me recover from the events of the day before.

Chapter 22

It was the night before the election, and the stage was set. Tonight's live, televised debate would move the undecided voters to one candidate or the other. There was general agreement that the voters who had already decided were probably not going to switch. Supporters of both candidates were passionate about their man. It would take a major blunder by one of the candidates to cause a supporter to move to the other side. The latest poll still had the candidates in a dead heat, with only four percent of the voters declaring themselves to be undecided.

Laura and I had been invited by Dennis Davis to be part of the studio audience. We chose, instead, to watch from the comfort of my living room. The debate was to begin at 7:00 p.m., only five minutes from now. The aroma of fresh popcorn just out of the microwave filled the room. Two ginger ales were parked on the coffee table, in front of the sofa.

At the appointed hour, the words "WLBT Special Presentation" appeared on the screen. I pointed the remote control at the television, and increased the volume. Patriotic music welcomed us to a set, where a small audience faced three tables, one in front of a trio of people, one in front of a single individual, and one that was vacant.

As the music faded, Walter B. Fox and Timothy Tyler appeared from behind the set, walked forward and took their seats side-by-side behind the vacant table that was draped with blue cloth. Tyler was wearing a dark blue suit with red tie. Fox had on a charcoal suit with red, white and blue striped tie. He was carrying a yellow legal pad in his left hand. Both candidates appeared to be relaxed and comfortable. Brett Foreman, the station's gravelly-voiced senior political affairs correspondent, began speaking into the camera.

"Good evening, ladies and gentlemen. I'm Brett Foreman, and with me, to my left are Ron Hardley with the Universal Press; Daniel Keesler with the *Clarion-Ledger;* and Greg Fields with Mississippi News Network. Tonight, the night before the voters of Jackson choose their next mayor, we are presenting this live debate in the hope that you, the voter, will be able to make as fully informed a decision as possible tomorrow, when you step inside the voting booth. It will be sixty minutes of uninterrupted discussion, free of commercials.

"The format of the debate will be as follows: The candidates will have five minutes each, for an opening statement. Then, each panelist will ask one question, which will be answered by each candidate. The response is limited to two minutes each. Following that, we will have a dialogue-type question and answer period, in which each panelist asks a direct question, then a follow-up to each candidate. The candidates will then have five minutes each, for a closing statement. Assuming that everyone understands the rules, let's begin with the opening comments of Walter B. Fox."

As Foreman shifted toward the candidate, so did the eyes of everyone in the studio. Fox placed the legal pad directly in front of him, and turned over the first page. He glanced to his immediate left, and received an affirmative nod from Tyler.

"Well, Brett," he began, "I'm afraid that there is not going to be much of a debate tonight."

Fox looked across at Foreman, who looked sideways at the panelists. Laura leaned forward and said, "Oh, my God. He's flipped out."

"You see," Fox continued, "this race has caused the candidates to become fully aware of the divisions that currently exist in Jackson. In some ways, this campaign has played on those divisions. And that is not good." He paused, raised his chin, and looked directly into the camera—into the eyes of thousands of Jacksonians who were now hanging on every word. "The real difference among people in Jackson is not between black and white, rich and poor, or those who live in the city and those in the suburbs. The real difference is among those who have something we call hope, and those who have no hope. Those of us who have hope for this community will, we believe, be judged by what we do for those who have no hope.

"This campaign has shown the candidates that only by working together, can we provide that hope. Therefore, Mr. Tyler and I met this afternoon, and reached an agreement, which Mr. Tyler will read to you now."

At that precise moment a blanket of attention fell over Jackson. There was a sense that something big was about to happen. Laura reached over and held my hand. Both of us leaned forward. The camera switched to Tyler, who accepted the yellow pad from Fox, and began reading from it as the camera lens zoomed in for a full-face shot.

"We, Walter B. Fox and Timothy Tyler, believe that it is in the best interests of the citizens of Jackson for us to work together toward the common good. We believe the citizens are tired of public officials who bicker with each other, and place their own desires ahead of the wishes and needs of the community.

"Therefore, we have agreed, that if Walter Fox is elected mayor tomorrow, one of his first acts will be to create the position of Deputy Mayor, and appoint Timothy Tyler thereto. Likewise, if Timothy Tyler is elected mayor, he will appoint Walter Fox to the position of Deputy Mayor.

"We now ask all of the registered voters to go to the polls tomorrow and exercise their right to vote. Thank you."

They both stood up and walked back off the set into the darkness from which they had come. The camera moved back to a full-face view of a stunned Brett Foreman. He could only manage to say, "We—uhh—will be right back after this commercial message."

Chapter 23

Thirty minutes after "The Debate" ended, Laura and I entered the large, rounded foyer of Dennery's Restaurant, with its framed photographs of the famous who had dined at this Jackson culinary landmark. I asked the attractive hostess behind the podium for a table for two by the fountain. While waiting, we surveyed the wall of photographs, and discovered images of such luminaries as former President Ronald Reagan, race car driver Dale Earnhardt, entertainer Jerry Clower, and Jackson's own grammy award-winning Dorothy Moore.

"One day, you might be on that wall if you keep solving high-profile cases," said Laura, with a grin and a nudge of her elbow to my ribcage.

A female voice directed at us said, "Right this way, Mr. Boulder," and we were led by the hostess to a table beside a flowing fountain surrounded by Greek columns in the center of the main dining room. We placed our orders, then indulged in salted crackers topped with some of the best salad dressing east of the Mississippi. Many of Dennery's customers buy it by the bottle, for use at the dinner table at home. I began to make a mental note to buy a bottle to take home, then thought better of it. I reached in my pocket, pulled out a palm-sized spiral ring notebook, and retrieved a pen from my shirt pocket.

"What are you doing?" asked Laura.

"You know how I'm always making mental notes to do things?"

"And then never get around to doing them?" she commented teasingly.

"Well, I'm starting a new system when I have one of those mental notes to make. I just put it in here, and it becomes a written note. That way, I can refer to it and just check it off."

I opened the cover, and added "Dennery's dressing" to the list.

"Mind if I see your notes?" she asked.

"Not at all," I said, handing her the notebook.

"Umm. Some of these look rather interesting. Train to New Orleans. Fairview Inn. What does this one mean?" she asked, pointing to an entry on the first page. "Pay one slash two four be four?"

"Remember the police officer who got shot by the guy in the back of the van? He has a wife and two small kids. Chief Dallas is setting up an education fund for the children. I'm going to donate one-half of my fee from the Jackson Business Association to that fund."

"That's a nice gesture," she said.

Two glasses of red wine arrived. As we sipped the scarlet water, we reminisced over the events of the past week, and became philosophical in the process. The fountain made its gurgling music beside us.

"Jack," she asked, becoming very still, " are you glad

you moved back to Jackson?"

"I sure am," I replied, gazing into her eyes. We raised our glasses and clinked a toast. "After all, this is the crossroads of the sunny, sunny South, the capital of the Magnolia State and the home of women like Laura Webster. You can't go wrong in Jackson."